i

Mind Games

How it All Began

For my friend Gayle, who enjoys the screen and stage; a writer who causes me to appreciate kind, thoughtful people in this life.

The IPM Corporation offered instruction empowering many of us to become self-reflective, critical thinkers with the skill set necessary to leverage the psychological momentum of others. Because of the invaluable ways in which we became empowered, we achieved great accomplishments and shaped the future of a brighter world. May we always continue to engage others with mind games!

Mind Games

How it All Began

Book One

Genre: Action adventure, fiction
"Real Stories" = "real fiction"

Library of Congress Data
Goodwin, Adam
Mind Games : How it All Began, First Edition
Copyright 2017
Second Edition
ISBN: 9798582354888

Contents

The Plain Truth about Mind Games

This work, in its entirety, is the product of the imagination of the author. Readers should not make any assumptions regarding the existence of an actual company represented by the fictitious "Ambercrombie Relations Associates" also referenced as "ARA" or the "International Pen Manufacturing Corporation" also referenced as "IPM" or any other organization mentioned herein. All seeming similarities between the people I discuss and genuine individuals, newsworthy historical events, or actual occurrences should be considered as purely coincidental. This work should be regarded as completely fictional entertainment. Some of the towns, cities, and schools named are actual places, provided solely in the interest to give a context for the telling of the story. Other than that, if you choose to believe that any part of this is true or make the erroneous assumption that one of these stories is about you or someone you know, then you are wrong. Every character mentioned herein is the fictional creation of the mind of the author. No matter what you read ahead, the evidence you think you've found, or how compelling the writing of these stories may become, please do not let yourself be duped as the victim of a mind game. Nothing you will read within the pages of this book is true, with the exceptions of the copyright page, the ISBN, this statement, and the next paragraph. No other part of this composition is factual, historically reliable, or true.

Special Thanks

I have a great wife and that's a vast understatement. Thank you, sweetheart, for giving me the time to write this book. You are wonderful, and I am so grateful for your loving support, kind encouragement, and critical caring reflections. I could not have told what needed to be said without you. My only regret in this life will have been my inability to fully express my love for you and the darling who knew me as "Tease."

I remain humbled to have been born into the Martin Clan. Our legacy is awesome, and I felt it was necessary to preserve some of it here. Despite our shortcomings, we've always had one another's backs. We have been exciting neighbors, defenders of the kin and protectors of the hood.

I will always be, indebted to Dr. Elias Jefferson, a.k.a. "Pete Sommers," "Alvin Brash," and a host of other identities. You provided me with an adventurous path through life, training me in the art of affecting and altering the minds, decisions, and actions of others.

The IPM Corporation offered instruction empowering many of us to become self-reflective, critical thinkers with the skill set necessary to leverage the psychological momentum of others. Because of the invaluable ways in which we became empowered, we achieved great accomplishments and shaped the future of a brighter world. May we always continue to engage others with mind games!

The Backstory of Mind Games

The stories you are about to read are real. The decision to write these down came from a guy I'll reference as "Old Brass." He was an associate with military intelligence connections who had suspicions about my past. He warned me, "I've checked out every detail of your existence!"

I ruminated over his assertion for a day and began to wonder about the accuracy of his intel. Finally, I became curious to know what his resources might have discovered. Had the tracks of my former life been thoroughly covered? After gaining the assurance that my secret past identity and life were safe, I lamented that the valuable work of IPM should not merely be swept under the rug to be lost and forgotten. The ways in which participants were transformed, the methods we learned, and the strategies we practiced profoundly altered the world. Eventually, despite the dangers putting this in print might cause, for the sake of posterity, I was compelled to bring these concerns back to life.

I don't know how my former associates will react to the revealing of this material and remain uncertain about who still may be looking over my shoulder. Therefore, it has been necessary for me to prioritize the release of the information contained herein. If the publications suddenly end, it may in fact be the result of having to run once again...or worse.

As you join me in the adventure of a life from days now passed, I hope that the narrative ahead provides a means of self-reflection and that your being will be re-shaped so that you make the world around you a better place. Peace!

Welcome to Mind Games and Enjoy!!!

Dedicated to the loving memory of Wendell Michael Martin

These Are the Real Stories

How it All Began

Prologue

When I woke up, I couldn't see, and I discovered immediately that my hands were tied behind my back. Something covered my head, and I heard what sounded like an exotic bird cawing. Several broken recollections flooded my mind, including the voice of Sharon Baxter remarking, "He who laughs first, laughs last." The pain that racked my body provided ample evidence that she'd definitely gotten the better of me.

Had I been asleep for days? My mind was like peanut butter; sticky, sticky peanut butter. My last memories seemed to have originated more than a year ago. How long had I been out? Was I dreaming? Where was I?

Gradually, it came to me. I was in trouble. I remembered giving the folks at IPM a run for their money. I warned them, "Your building is surrounded." Did I sound like the punk as I had intended? They weren't willing to negotiate, although I'd offered the opportunity.

Something covered my head, and I asked blindly, "Dr. Jefferson? Are you here?" Silence and darkness surrounded me. Except for the sound of tropical birds and wind, I was outside and alone; laid over sideways on a sandy, gravel road. It smelled wet and dank. I fidgeted to get my hands free when I heard the first voice. My head was too cloudy to make out what he was saying.

After a few moments, there were several individuals gathered around, speaking all at once. Perhaps to see if I was alive, one or more of them kicked me. Then, someone began shouting orders, and I realized they conversed in a language I couldn't understand. I later discovered that it was a mutual problem. "Is Jack Strauss here?" I asked. I was coming to my senses.

They left me tied up and dragged me onto a piece of wood. Hot trickles of sweat ran down my forehead, neck, back, arms, and stomach. Then, they lifted one end and began pulling me down a gravel road. Where was I? The hinges of a creaky door or gate opened, and I had the sense that they were taking me inside. No, I was mistaken. We'd passed through a shaded area, but moments later, we were still outside and back in the sun.

I vaguely recollected a far-off conversation about "trial by ordeal." What was that all about? Then, I remembered the blurry view of Old Baldy. He was in charge, and they were going to test me to determine if I was a mole. He pointed at me and said "Bangkok." Some of it was beginning to come back. Was this really Southeast Asia?

I thought about Baxter's snide proclamation once more. It meant that a person who thought they had won, in fact, was premature in his conclusion. She got the last laugh on me when she forcefully jabbed a needle into my left arm. What had I remarked about her boyfriend? The woman had taken me by surprise. Then, I became weak and let myself feebly down to the floor of the office. Everything went quiet and dark. What had I said about Durlong? Did I screw things up? It was impossible to put all my thoughts and memories back together. This is how it all began.

Axiom One
Boys are stupid.

Remember the start of the Wizard of Oz? It was vital for Dorothy to begin her journey at the start of the Yellow Brick Road. Well, it's the same here. The window into my life, one filled with intrigue, passion, deception, untold millions of dollars' worth of destruction, years of training as an assassin, and the demise of innumerable individuals has very much to do with my childhood. If you understand who I was in my formative years, the inclinations, eventualities, and accomplishments of my adult life will make much more sense. Without further ado, we'll start with my identity during high school.

I tried to teach my daughters that "boys are stupid." I knew it was a trustworthy statement, because it was conceived in self-reflection. Boys and men, who haven't yet realized that they're stuck in pre-adolescence, do all kinds of wild things they think are funny that wind up getting them into trouble. They make ridiculous choices, create loads of problems for others, and drive half the world around them crazy.

This is because of the limited growth of the frontal lobe of their brains; so, I later learned in child development classes half a lifetime later. This part of the brain foresees consequences and plans accordingly. It calls all other behavior and potential decisions into check; by re-funneling what are initially thought of as "bright ideas" back through the cerebral processes for reconsideration.

The frontal lobe tames that which otherwise remains uncontrolled and is destined to wreak havoc. It is the sentinel of thought and livelihood; whose existence revolves around the hope of determining safer, more reliable solutions, and practical navigation through life. Basically, this cranial feature curbs stupidity. In boys it develops much more slowly than in girls.

Problematically, at the time young men need it most, between the ages of six and twenty, for the most part, it's a dormant mass of gray matter. For the very unlucky, even as adults, it may be that this vital facet of cognition remains missing altogether.

Axiom Two
Be careful who you trust.

As a senior in Bodega High School, I was a student in Mrs. Berry's study hall. She trusted me implicitly, having been convinced that *Mr. Levi Martin* was one of those good students. Whether or not that was actually the case, all that mattered to me was maintaining her perception in order to gain privileges.

Despite the deficits in my vastly underdeveloped frontal lobe, one thing was certain, some parts of my mind worked just fine. I now realize that my strongest abilities and thinking processes didn't foster the kinds of strengths people usually brag about on a resume. But, if they were, I'd have championed over others as one of the most talented liars, cheaters, and stealers roaming the beaches of Bodega, California. In my family, those were the characteristics necessary for survival, and I was determined to survive.

Deep inside I was shrewd and conniving. If any goal came to mind, I couldn't rest until I devised a means of obtaining the

4

object of my concern. It's probably why I've never slept well, not then or even now. Once pressed into action, my cerebral processes will stop at nothing to determine the most workable solution to a problem.

The mission at hand was to find a way out of study hall. The proper contrite looking facial expression and tone of voice were stepping stones toward success. Tim and I were headed for relative freedom in the library, and I had something secret to show him.

Mrs. Berry looked down speaking as she completed our hall passes.

"So, are you boys preparing for an exam?"

Her voice was sweet as she briefly smiled up at us.

I lied, "Yes, ma'am. Thank you very much."

My intonation spoke volumes, affirming that she alone was kind enough in her judicious demonstration of authority to permit us to leave the mundane class in order to better ourselves academically. She handed me the ticket to freedom and wrote another for Tim.

For at least the first half of my life, along with my younger brother, Wendell, I proved that I could be a tried and true hellion on the outside, who appeared in most contexts of life to be innocent as a dove.

The little light-yellow paper, containing Mrs. Berry's signature, would prevent questions and harassment in the hall on the way downstairs. Without the small protective shield, authority figures who discovered that your whereabouts weren't properly sanctioned might send you to after-school detention or worse. A wise student flittered the pastel form so that it could be seen openly, thereby ensuring undisturbed arrival at his destination.

Students with foresight learned to keep these discrete passports to independence for reuse. With a good eraser and talented doctoring, older passes served almost perpetually as tools for the misdirection of attention and the subversion of authority.

While waiting for the completion of Tim's pass, I walked around behind Mrs. Berry, tore mine into a hundred tiny pieces and sprinkled these into her hair. It may be difficult to believe I was such a complete idiot, but that's exactly what I did. When I was little, I'd once overheard an uncle comment that he didn't think I was the sharpest ax in the woodshed. To be blunt about it, Levi Martin was just plain stupid. In those days, my frontal lobe must have been half the size of a lima bean.

"Thanks, so much, Mrs. Berry!" Tim said with a wink, as we gathered our books and made our exit.

Thirty minutes later, we were sitting on the floor between the library book racks, hiding from supervision and devising trouble. It was completely unexpected, but there, walking past the end of the biography section, heading toward the cubicles in the back of the study area, was Mrs. Berry; storming by with an infuriated look on her face. It wasn't until that very moment that I had any idea how stupid my actions were and realized how much trouble I was in. There would be even worse problems for both of us if she didn't find us in the library, fairly quickly.

Had she found the paper sprinkled in her bouffant hairdo? Only someone as stupid as me needed to wonder.

One thing was certain, I had to take action before this became a matter involving Mom. My rear end couldn't afford a call home. Mom could either be the most loving, angelic being on this side of heaven or prove herself as the indomitable whip. She used to threaten, "If I get a call from that school, I'll tear your arm off and beat you to death with the bloody limb!"

Both Mom and Dad meant business when it came to doling out tangible and unforgettable means of loving discipline. It usually began with the default statement, "Get the belt." None of us wanted to hear those words. Look out when you did!

I caught our teacher's attention, feebly asking, "Mrs. Berry?"

Axiom Three
Doing what is right and true provides a safety net in life.
Acquire virtue and integrity.

I'm not proud of myself for my values and the kinds of choices I made during this phase of my life. I once heard a wise person say, "Humility is being known for who you are." I like to think that the person I eventually became was mostly a decent citizen, a likable neighbor, and a valued ally. At the start of my life, however, it was a different story.

Contraband I'd acquired was the reason Tim and I were hiding between the book racks. It was hidden in the folder my friend happened to be holding when Mrs. Berry stood looking over us with indignation. The smile fled from Tim's face as he closed his notebook over the forbidden material and handed it back to me. He was relieved to safely rid himself of the hot potato.

If I had a working frontal lobe, I'd have casually slid all of it between some books on the shelf when we stood up.

I hadn't yet told Tim about my pass, so he thought we were in trouble for what he'd been holding. She marched us into the hall, and as the pieces of the puzzle were reassembled, through the discussion that took place, my friend realized that he was probably safe. However, I had much to lose and envisioned Mom getting the fateful call and Dad finding my bludgeoned, armless body outside our house on the lawn.

Axiom Four
Desperate people pray desperately.

It was in situations like these where I think I also learned about the practical value of heartfelt, desperate prayer. "Oh Lord, please help me!" was a phrase that whispered forth from between my lips on many occasions. It was frequently followed by, "Please get me out of this!"

If there were two things I'd learned on just about every Sunday morning at Bodega Second Baptist, these were that I didn't want to go to hell, and the Almighty answered sincere heartfelt prayer.

This may be nearly impossible for anybody to believe, although Tim was my witness, I was actually able to talk myself out of the disrespect of Mrs. Berry without any form of punishment whatsoever. If I'd ever been endowed with any gift at all, it was the unmistakable talent of talking myself out of almost any problem in the world; that's unless it involved a phone call home to Mom. The ability was undoubtedly a sign of the Almighty's merciful intervention in my life and the reward of excellent Sunday school attendance. There was no trip to the principal's office, no detention, and thank the Lord, no call home. Indeed, he was with me!

After all was said and done, I can only imagine that Mrs. Berry took pity because she realized what a hopeless and pathetically stupid boy I was.

The quality of being able to squirm out of tricky situations was something that later in the next year as a college freshman, caught the attention of the recruiters for IPM. Half a decade later, when I began full-time work in Paramus, I frequently overheard comments like:

"Levi is something else!"

"He deserved to get caught, and I thought they were going to nail him."

"How the heck did he get out of that one?"

Honestly, often my elusion of authority and enemies, while working with IPM, was just a plain miracle. I can't take credit for all of those renowned escapes based on my skills alone. In a few instances, I received clandestine help from others. It will be a while before I can elaborate with examples.

Before I'd actually been accepted into their ranks and was still labeled as a rogue punk on their radar, I earned the nickname "Houdini." However cool or infamous the label sounded, it was a double-edged sword. Some of the folks at IPM proved to be very jealous and treated me spitefully; even after years of service.

"They call him 'Houdini' because Levi escaped a decade of work proving that he was as dedicated and trustworthy as the rest of us."

"He's always up to something."

"We just can't trust that guy!"

Some of them were much harder on me; particularly the complementary gender. I learned from Sharon and Aubrey that once you'd ticked them off that was it forever. Those women, especially Aubrey, relentlessly poked, prodded, insulted, and made my existence at IPM miserable; every moment and chance they had. Pastor James used to teach, "Forgiveness becomes more than a theory, only when you have to exercise it with someone who really hurts you." He taught that the Almighty wouldn't forgive us if we didn't forgive others. I have to admit that it was pretty challenging for me to put up with Aubrey's never ending, malicious antics, and so, repeatedly, I found myself praying, "Help me to forgive her Lord and to really mean it."

In some senses, the crew were more than mere co-workers. They were also my prey, and in concerted moments of need, I worked on their psyches relentlessly; partially because I'd been forced to do it. I wasn't an innately evil person. They never knew about the race for my own survival. I carried a few pretty big burdens. Some of the IPMers, who hated me most, had no idea that my efforts extended their lives. I also knew that they'd never know me long enough to say, "Thanks!" It's a complicated story, and I hope to be able to explain all of it in a way that makes sense. Almost from the day, I got in, I tried to find my way out. I lived an extreme life, walking a tenuous tightrope, eventually, praying to find freedom as I had that miraculous day with Mrs. Berry. The Almighty has rescued me repeatedly. Nevertheless, to this very day, I keep vigilant watch over my shoulder as a reflexive, survival instinct.

Axiom Five

Fiercly protect those who are precious in your life.

Undoubtedly, it was Mom who had the largest influence in my life. I still recall the moment as if it were yesterday. My little brother and I had arrived home from the pool and we were terrified having heard Mom hollering and shouting so loudly behind the closed door of her bedroom that the walls were shaking. Dad was already at work, Kathy was outside playing, and so we were at a loss at who else could have been in there. Somebody was getting slaughtered, and it turned out to be the devil. Mom was raising such a commotion we thought the roof would fall in. She was in a rage and nobody was getting out of there alive!

We crept toward the hallway and heard, "Get your filthy, thieving hands off my children! Shut your lying mouth! Their destiny is for blessing and not curse! I bind you devil in the name of the Almighty and cast you back into the pit of hell! You will get your hands off my boys in the name of the Son of God. I loose the angels of heaven in the name of the Almighty to lead Wendell, Levi, and Kathy in the ways of righteousness and to help them overcome the temptations of this world. Set them in the direction of pursuits that are true! I declare that they are bound to a future of obedience to the Almighty and that they will bring goodness and not harm into this world. They will embrace destinies of hope as your children and will know the way of peace. They will find joy and satisfaction in life!"

We were completely bewildered. Neither of us ever knew who it was that had taught Mom to pray shouting like that and marching around, but one thing was certain. She was full of fire and wasn't going to let anything from hell lay a hand on her family.

Axiom Five & ½
Rivalry may be healthy in some instances,
but not when fire is involved.

Wendell was my younger brother. He could be as mean and ornery as any Martin in the clan. Sometimes, we were the best of buds and other times we were the greatest of rivals. One day I set a model battleship on fire, which I partially blew up with miniature firecrackers called "lady fingers." I dabbed highly flammable model cement over parts of the hull, which acted like napalm. I lit up the ship with the stolen metal cased lighter that I'd always kept hidden in my sock. It was a sight to see with flames of every beautiful color. I stared and challenged Wendell, "Top that!" Fifteen minutes later, there were sirens in the street.

Several weeks earlier, the neighbors had left a sofa out by the curb for trash pickup. Wendell had used gasoline to set it on fire. What he hadn't anticipated was that the creosote-soaked telephone pole would also go up in flames. Our power was out for two days. That night before bed, I conceded, "You won this time, but remember, I'm still the big brother in this house!"

Some might say Wendell acted bizarre. He always had an extreme fear of failure, which was probably why he did so well in competition. He'd spend days, weeks, and months practicing for any kind of performance. My little brother was nuts.

Dad had lined us up before bed and asked, "What do you two know about the fire today?" By then, we'd had plenty of time to formulate a convincing alibi. Wendell soberly lied, "We were at the pool."

I added, "When we came back we saw the fire trucks!"

At least it was half true. We'd walked our bikes through the backyard amidst the mayhem and disappeared down to the Bodega Park Recreational Center.

Mom came in and confirmed, "Honey, the boy's wet swimsuits, and towels are in the laundry room and smell like chlorine."

It was smart to plant evidence to support our fabricated story. We'd learned much about avoiding punishment as we grew up, listening to Dad's tales with our uncles.

To understand the Martin Clan, it's necessary to realize that items any of us could burn were like potential friends. Possessions we could blow up were practically family. No greater joy came from anything except experiences that culminated in sparks, explosions, and infernos.

I'd learned just prior to entering high school that "Adara" meant "fire" in Hebrew. She was my true love in more ways than one. To whisper "A~dar~ah" mesmerized me while staring into the depths of the interwoven flames. Adara was alive and I was awestruck with her beauty. She spoke to me through the crackling, while her sparks lit up my heart.

I replied, "Yes, love, I hear your sweet darling voice."

The first time Wendell heard me chant the mantra and speak to the flames, he informed me, "You're nuts!"

My simple reply was, "Oh yeah, what kind of a guy gives a name to his soccer ball?" Besides, he didn't actually know the real secret of the term's significance. I always thought he should know, and it was probably the only thing I ever kept from him, until one day my little brother was suddenly gone from our lives.

Wendell frequently conversed with "Ducco," to the extent that he'd embarrass us in public settings!

I was proud of myself for knowing a Hebrew term when I was just fourteen years of age. My heart aches to begin by telling the full story of Adara and her vast significance in my life, but, it will take an entire book. I should stick to the priority of the mission. Here and now, I'm compelled to begin mainly with my formative years leading up to college and my recruitment into IPM.

Adara, my love, please forgive me. You must wait for now, until the story of our love can be told in full!

Axiom Six
Remember your childhood fibbing stories.

An important component of the Martin heritage had to do with fibbing. This was a regular practice we associated with having fun. Most of what we enjoyed wasn't allowed, therefore, evading questions regarding one's actions necessitated fabrication of new realities. Because parents make legalistic judgments for their kids, it's necessary to figure out how to navigate a way around the rules.

We were driving down the road one day, and I was probably five years old. While sitting in the back seat of the Chevrolet and pondering my existence, the thought occurred to me, "Parents swear frequently, but kids are never allowed to say those things. Why?" So, I tested the water and said a very, very, bad word. I'd heard that one on Dad's construction site but had never tried it out for myself.

"&%#@$!"

My parents abruptly quit talking. Dad looked up into the rearview mirror and asked, "What did you just say?"

14

With enthusiasm, I repeated, "&%#@$!"

Immediately, Dad laid heavy on the brakes and pulled hard to the curb. He glared back over the seat.

Mom whispered in his ear, "I don't think he knows what it means!"

Who's gonna' explain to Moms that whispering to Dads in the close confines of a parked car doesn't work? I gratefully inferred from her comment that some things were best kept private; like "&%#@$!"

"Do you know what that word means?" Dad demanded.

"Nope!" I fibbed.

He was silent for a moment and looked at Mom, then studied my face. "Well listen to me, young man. You're not allowed to say that word anymore! Alright?"

"Okay!"

The practical value of denial saved me from a whipping. I'm not sure how it was that my Martin cousins figured it out for themselves, but all of us knew how to change the facts, embellish a story, and how to invent an alibi to get out of trouble.

There were lots of double standards between grownups and youngsters, but it was possible to level the playing field with a fib. If I engaged in illicit activities, I could use the tool to cover my tracks. So long as Mom and Dad lived in the imaginary world of my lies, I could pretty much do whatever I pleased. It's important for a little guy to get this figured out before too much of life passes him by!

"Are you fibbing to me?" Mom would ask from time to time.

"Nope!" was the only rational reply. I mean, what the heck did she expect me to say? "Yep!" and "Should I go get you the bar of soap?"

I was probably in about 6th grade when I realized that lies weren't only useful evasive devices but were also effective tools for manipulation. A good lie at just the right moment could cause your adversary to make a decision that might come back to haunt him. The problem, however, was that I could just as easily become the victim of someone else's evil intentions.

Lies became the commerce of relationship amongst my cousins. We gained infamy each time we managed to trick one another into doing something they'd have to lie their way out of. Therefore, we always tried our best to remain wary to protect ourselves.

Axiom Seven
Don't play with fire when Mom or Dad are home.

One evening, I was holding my lighter in one hand and a string of firecrackers in the other. Wendell and I stood in our bedroom and I looked at the open window and said, "Dare me?"

He said, "Yeah!"

I lit the explosives and chucked them out toward the front yard. Instead of launching out the window, as intended, they hit the edge of the frame and bounced back into the room. Unfortunately for us, they landed squarely inside the shoebox full of fireworks. Everything went off in the next minute. The room was filled with thick yellow smoke and we quickly stamped out the burning shards of cardboard that threatened the curtains and covers on our beds.

I scolded the flames, "Adara! You've betrayed us! How dare you!" Adara was tricky. You had to keep your eye on her. She'd rob you and laugh. She was a tease. As was the case so many other times, once again, she'd gotten out of hand and lured us into a load of trouble!

We heard the stampede of Mom and Dad's feet up the stairs and down the hall. Wendell said, "Fast! In here!" He shoved me into the closet and pulled the door shut. We peeked out through the crack and saw the hallway door swing open.

As our parents were enveloped in a thick yellow cloud of smoke, Dad's angry, booming voice demanded, "What in the hell is going on?"

I thought I might just pee my pants! We stood frozen in the dark; not even breathing, straining wide-eyed to see one another. Mom seemed to know about our hiding place and swooshed the closet door open. There we stood, guilty as sin. Before either of them could say a word, Wendell and I both began shouting.

"Levi did it!"

"Wendell dared me!"

"It's his fault!"

"It was his idea!"

Dad clarified everything, "I don't give a damn who did what!" Then, he commenced altering the shape and color of our rear ends with his belt. About an hour later we both stood at the kitchen counter eating our macaroni and cheese dinner because neither of us could sit down. The entire house smelled like burnt sulfur for weeks.

Axiom Eight
Prove you really care by making trouble.

The Martin Clan used to trade kids. For a month or six weeks in the summer, Wendell or I would be sent off to Arizona or New Mexico. One of our other cousins would come to stay with us. It was cool because our friends thought it was weird. Sometimes it was a three-way trade. I'd go to Eddie's, Eddie would go to Robert's, and Robert would come to our house. Staying at home had its benefits due to home-court-advantage. In my own backyard, I knew the ropes and was less likely to get caught up in some scheme designed to get me into trouble. Instead, it was easier to set up one of my cousins.

Wendell and I were at Stewart's one summer when he suggested, "Hey guys, let's play ding-dong-ditch-it." You'd ring some guy's doorbell and then run.

The real goal of the evening, however, was to get someone so turned around that he didn't know his way back home. Then, you'd try to get him caught by some neighbor who you knew could run fast.

"Okay, Levi. It's your turn." Stewart slapped me on the shoulder and smiled. We'd been having a blast at this all night, and now, it was dark. I rang the doorbell and turned to run away with Stewart, Eddie, and Wendell, but they had already disappeared. Feeling stunned, I fled to the corner of the guy's yard and ditched it under the low branches of a pine tree. I glanced around and whispered, "Hey you guys! Come on!" It finally dawned on me that I was all alone. They were probably off in the distance laughing at me and I began to wonder to myself, which way is home?

All the while, the guy was out on his front porch hollering and threatening to kill whoever it was that pulled the prank. It was stressful enough being left behind in the dark of night, but now to also hear how this man intended to tear me limb from limb was a lot to deal with.

We'd hit between five and seven streets, until we were several blocks away. If you really did things right, you could get your cousin lost so he couldn't find his way back to your house.

In our families, your aunts and uncles were just as likely to spank you as your own parents.

"And you know, if he needs it, you let him have it!"

Frequently, those were the departing instructions shared between our parents.

I knew if I didn't find my way back before bedtime that I'd get the belt from Uncle Raymond. I could imagine Stewart's tattletale voice, "Yeah, Dad, we told Levi not to take off on us, but you know how he is." Eddie would shake his head in agreement precipitating the final judgment and eventual spanking. My cousins would have a good laugh about the whole thing.

Axiom Nine
Careful premeditation works best.

Setting someone up was a two-way street. Once, I visited Eddie's house and took a few items out of the drawer next to Uncle Raymond's bed. I gave him two full weeks to stew about his missing possessions.

Timing was everything, so I waited until the day after Eddie got me in trouble for taking the cookies above the fridge. He told me they were fair game. After I'd enjoyed them with a tall glass of milk, he lied to his Mom that I'd been warned not to eat them. I got the belt.

One afternoon, he was at swimming lessons and Aunt Edna had asked for my help taking the sheets off the beds for the laundry. Really fast, I took the stash of Uncle Raymond's belongings that I'd hidden behind the record player and put all of them between Eddie's mattresses; along with some other contraband I knew he didn't want her to find. Then, I called her into my cousin's room.

"What is it, Levi?"

I pointed up at the frame on the wall, asking, "Where were you guys at when you had this picture taken?"

As she began explaining, I pulled the sheet from between the mattresses, and several items fell to the floor.

I pretended to be unaware, but she looked down questioning, "What's all this?"

"I don't know, ma'am. I was just getting these sheets off here like you asked."

She lifted up the mattress and a few more artifacts slid out, landing at her feet.

"Really? Let me have a closer look."

I lifted the other corner of my cousin's mattress, where I'd added a few accessories that I'd stolen from their neighbor's house along with a few of Eddie's pocket toys.

Aunt Edna's stern tone of voice announced, "Okay, Levi, just leave all these things alone. Eddie and I are going to have a little talk when he gets back from the pool."

"A little talk" was grown up code meaning my cousin was destined to get his butt whipped.

A set up had to appear convincing. The whole scheme never would've worked if I'd supposedly found all these things on my own and finked on him. That would've made me a suspect too. Instead, I'd turned his Mom into a material witness. Her own discovery became part of the evidence that would result in sentencing with the belt.

Of course, my cousin attempted to deny everything, arguing, "Holy cow, Mom, I've never seen that gold lighter before in my life!"

He was actually telling the truth.

She replied tersely, "I suppose you've never seen any of the rest of these things before either? Take off your belt!"

Although he pled with her, the impending punishment was swift and certain. He held back for a moment, as tears welled up in his eyes.

Finally, Aunt Edna demanded, "Give me your belt right now, or you're gonna' get it worse!" As Eddie prepared for the inevitable, she commented, "And we're going to find out whose initials are engraved on that lighter and you're going to return it and apologize. If you don't tell me where you got it, you're going to get it again when I figure it out." She read the engraving aloud, "P.L.M.," demanding, "Who does this belong to?"

My cousin was already crying before the spanking began, "I don't know, Mom, I don't know!"

"WHAP!" "WHAP!" "WHAP!" "WHAP!" "WHAP!"

When Uncle Raymond got home from work and saw the collection of missing items on the kitchen table, there was a replay; but this time with his Dad's belt which was much worse.

"WHAP!" "WHAP!" "WHAP!" "WHAP!" "WHAP!"

The following evening when his parents figured out that "P.L.M." stood for "Patrick Logan Morton," the next-door neighbor, Eddie got it again in the man's living room. My cousin was forced into a false confession, "I'm sorry Mr. Morton. I don't know what I was thinking. I promise that I'll never take anything from your house ever again." His vow was sealed, in a triple jeopardy penalty with his own belt.

"WHAP!" "WHAP!" "WHAP!" "WHAP!" "WHAP!"

If you really loved your cousin, then you went to creative lengths to prove it. Eddie was the only cousin I ever got beat three different times for the same crime that he didn't commit. We continue to laugh about that one at family reunions, but, to this day, I keep a watchful eye over my shoulder.

Axiom Ten
Payback is bliss.

Cousin Fritz taught me how to pickpocket. You'd bump into a guy to distract him and nab his wallet or reach in his coat pocket and steal his lighter. Worse yet for our victim, we'd put some piece of contraband in his pocket and then get him into trouble for having it.

Joey Meyers was the neighborhood bully. He had the gall once to punch my sister Kathy for the crime of riding her bike on, what he said was, "his side of the street." Dad raised us with the clear understanding that you never dare hit a girl or disrespect her in any way. Therefore, in our minds, what Joey did was unconscionable. Wendell freaked out and promised, "I'll kill the next guy that ever lays a hand on Kathy."

There was no end to the trouble Joey caused for kids smaller and weaker than himself in the hood or at school. The

22

problem was that the kid was three times the size of any other boy his age. He was almost as tall as our Dad. For his repeated crimes, Wendell and I committed several years to the project we labeled, "Goliath's Colossal Payback;" a retribution that included physical, emotional, and psychological torment.

For years, I lived with Pastor James' voice in my mind admonishing that we should've just forgiven Meyers and tried to be friends. Looking back, I don't know why that would've been so difficult. I still wince and ask the Almighty to forgive me, whenever I think of Joey.

One day, I saw Mrs. Urbanski's bracelet sitting on her desk a few feet away from where I sat. Joey Meyers had just turned in his quiz. I stepped up there fast to ask a question and put my paper over the jewelry. After having one of the sentences explained to me, I discretely snagged up the piece of treasure and went back to my seat. When we were rustling around the room putting reading material back on the shelf, I deposited the stolen item into Meyers' jacket pocket. Just before she let us out of class, I passed a note up to her desk that read, "I think Joey stole a bracelet off your desk when he turned in his exam." She held him after class, and the rest was history. Mr. Washington, our highly esteemed principal, who would've made a good linebacker for the San Francisco 49ers, let him have it good with the thick paddle that had the aerodynamic holes drilled through it.

Wendell and I learned that there was more than one way to take down a kid who was bigger and dumber. As we left school for the day, we saw Joey's Mom striding up the walkway. I bragged, "It looks like Meyers is going to get a second round!"

Our scheming and antics were addictive. We became legends at family gatherings as we secretly told stories to our cousins of what we'd gotten away with.

Axiom Eleven
Manipulate authority figures to take action on your behalf.

It was a big deal when we were kids if you had a candy bar. You were best off just eating it right when it came into your possession, because Mom might make you share it with everyone if she found out about it.

Wendell and I were staying at Uncle Mike and Aunt Jenny's. Little Mikey had cut grandpa's yard the day before and earned 25 cents, which he used to purchase a Three Musketeers Bar down at the corner store. It was the giant-sized bar, and we all became jealous as he flaunted it the next day.

Stewart, Eddie, and I were pretending to be his best friend hoping to score at least half.

Little Mikey used the situation to leverage us, "Anyone got any firecrackers and a lighter to trade for this?" He'd viciously slide it out of his hoodie pocket and squint his eyes, while we watched, salivated, and hoped to think of a worthy item with which to bargain. Mikey was a miniature control freak, and he loved the power that the candy bar gave him over us.

"What can we give him, Wendell? How about your bottle rockets?"

"Forget it, Levi. He's a fake! Mikey isn't going to share that with anyone!"

If you knew my brother, he was always off in his own world thinking three steps ahead of the rest of us conjuring a plan of his own. Aunt Jenny had taken us boys grocery shopping with her,

24

and several times along the way Mikey took out the candy bar and messed with us. We were in the store for about 10 minutes, when Wendell took action.

"Excuse me, sir."

My little brother tugged on the store manager's vest.

"Yes son, how can I help you?"

"Well, do you see that boy over there in the blue hooded sweatshirt?"

"Yes, what about him?"

"Well, before we came here, he was bragging about how he always steals candy when his Mom brings him in. He just stole a candy bar and it's in his pocket."

Aunt Jenny stopped shopping and listened to the store manager, then told Mikey, "Empty your pockets now, young man!"

He pulled out a collection of toys, along with the Three Musketeers bar. She pointed and demanded, "Give that back to the manager, and take off your belt!"

Mikey had such a look of betrayal on his face, he couldn't believe what was happening. He objected passionately, "But Mom, this is mine! I bought it at the corner store yesterday with the money gramps paid me for mowing the lawn!"

Aunt Jenny looked at Stewart, Eddie, and me, asking, "Well?"

We all shrugged, looked clueless, and replied together, "We've never seen that before ma'am."

Stewart added, "The corner store was already closed by the time we finished gramps' lawn."

She was firm with Mikey, "I want your belt this instant, and I better not hear another word!"

Our cousin got it right then and there in the bread aisle. "WHAP!" "WHAP!" "WHAP!" "WHAP!" "WHAP!" The chocolate bar that he actually owned went back on the shelf at the store. Then, because he'd embarrassed his Mom, he got it again, even worse, when his Dad got home. "WHAP!" "WHAP!" "WHAP!" "WHAP!" "WHAP!"

Wendell bragged to me later, "If I'd told Aunt Jenny that Mikey had stolen it, she might not have believed me. But, I knew if I spoke to that man, and he confronted Mikey's Mom, it would be the same as being caught red-handed."

Wendell was a smart cookie! I had to take care whenever I ticked him off. Everyone learned to look out for his vengeance. Even so, he had a special talent for making friends with the worst of rivals and enemies. He'd get their butts whooped and look all the better for it by everyone involved.

Later, he told us, "I used little Mikey's spanking as a diversion to steal a few of the prizes out of the cereal boxes over in the next aisle."

Only dignified and well-bonded cousins got each other's hides tanned.

Axiom Twelve
Don't get being stupid mixed up with fun.

My last year of high school, I had this friend named "Max" who lived in a constant state of trouble. When teachers found his name on their rosters, they received a complete dossier chocked full of information about his alleged and actual crimes. The ones who luckily missed out on having him in their classes held a party.

Max was a nuisance and lived as a constant suspect in the minds of administrators. His identity was synonymous with the

26

term "culprit." Even so, he was shrewd and kept many of his misdeeds just low enough below the proverbial radar zone, so that he could seldom be pinned down.

So, here I was on a different day with more contraband. And Max, a.k.a. "Trouble," thought it would be funny to put it on one of our teacher's world maps above the chalkboard.

The problem was that every time this instructor, Mr. Cline, went into the hallway, he locked the door behind him. Boy, was that guy smart! He understood the vast importance of detailed classroom management in light of students like me and Mr. Trouble with our pea-sized frontal lobes.

Axiom Thirteen
Effective people plan for success.
Prepare carefully!

So, Max and I came up with a bright idea. The school was U-shaped with a courtyard in the middle, and the first floor sat about four feet below the level of the lawn outside. Casement style windows swung out just inches above the grass. Because it was situated next to the ocean, the facility didn't need air conditioning. Accordingly, during the spring when it was nice outside, teachers often left these open for ventilation. Mr. Cline was no exception. At lunchtime, students also frequently played Frisbee in the courtyard.

While Cline was in the teacher's lounge, Max and I threw the Frisbee back and forth until we landed it right next to his opened window. We ran over and jumped down inside hoping nobody had noticed. Quickly pulling down the world map, we taped up the picture and made a hasty exit up over the bookshelves and back outside. It was hard to believe, but we had gotten away clean with the whole setup operation.

We expected to soon hear the scandalous news spreading throughout the school, but he didn't use the map again for the next two days. Oh, how the tension mounted in my soul! Unbelievably it wasn't until our own class, three days later, when the fateful moment occurred.

A girl was finishing her presentation, and I was up next to give my report on the Berlin Wall.

We sat in the back row, and Mr. Trouble was goading me under his breath, "Show us the location of Berlin when you get up there!"

I whispered, "No way man! There's no way I can pull down that map! I'll lose it up there in front of everybody! Absolutely not!"

As we engaged in the nearly silent quarrel, we suddenly heard the unmistakable flapping sound of the map rolling open at the front of the room.

We looked forward as Mr. Cline cried out, "Oh my gosh! Who did this?"

Axiom Fourteen
Getting away with it can be worse than getting caught.

There was a divine irony and poetic justice in the fact that I was up next to give my report. After all the commotion settled, I stood before my class, shaking in my boots. Sin rarely leaves the guilty untouched, and accordingly, as I walked forward to give my own presentation, paranoia convinced me that everyone in the room knew I was behind the whole thing.

Pastor James' voice in my mind admonished me that I should've known better. The very odds of the event occurring at this precise moment was a firm demonstration of the hand of the Almighty.

Culpability opens the door to invasive remorse, regret, and fear. These dynamic intellectual and emotional forces alter our perception and turn the world upside down.

Initially, I thought that our secret misdeed was going to be tremendously funny. Instead, I became the psychological victim of my own actions. As I struggled to explain a segment of Germany's history, I was enshrouded in a dark cloud, absolutely convinced the whole time that Mom and Dad would find out and kill me!

Axiom Fifteen
Endure hardship and celebrate survival.

When we were kids, Wendell and I got so many whippings that it's a wonder either of us could ever sit down. Red welts and pain were outward signs of the mischievous games and play that characterized our young lives.

"Got your butt whipped again today, Levi?"

"That's right, Wendell!"

We'd smile at one another, offer up a high-five and say together, "Evidence of the good life!" Then, we'd punch fists and I'd say, "Ya' gotta' have fun!" Wendell would respond, "Ya' gotta' get it done right!"

Every so often, we'd hear Mom's voice trailing from the kitchen, "*I'll show you two what fun is, and I'll get it done right! You're both either going to shape up or ship out!*"

One of the hardest things I ever had to do was keep a straight face when my brother or one of my cousins was getting

29

the belt for something I'd set up. If you were nearby, you didn't even dare crack a smile, or you might ruin it and incur worse punishment yourself.

Having heard Uncle Frank tell a story and reference something known as the "Claude Rains Effect," Wendell had a bright idea one day. The prank was named after the actor in the old action thriller, "The Invisible Man." Without telling our uncle's story now, suffice to say that the main point was that fishing line is nearly invisible and can be used for all kinds of pranks.

"Hey, Levi, does Dad have any spare fishing line in the tackle box?"

We went and looked but didn't find any.

"How much do you need, Wendell?"

"I think probably about ten feet or so."

We ended up cutting it off one of the poles in the garage.

"What are you up to?"

"I had an idea that if we could loop this around the toilet lever, then down around the back of the bowl, around the cabinet, and out under the door into the hall, when someone is sitting in there doing their business, we could pull the line and make the toilet flush."

I said, "That's hilarious. I've gotta' see this!"

We waited one Saturday for half the morning, until someone finally used the hall bathroom. Kathy went in, and we waited about 20 seconds for her to get seated. While Wendell knelt on the floor outside the bathroom door and yanked on the fishing line, I hid around the corner in our bedroom. Success! We heard the toilet flush and Kathy immediately began hollering. She didn't like being messed with.

We were cracking up laughing, until the door swooshed open, and she said, "I'm getting Mom!" Because it was a completely harmless joke, neither of us thought it would really matter. We sat there on the hall floor fully satisfied with the outcome of our mischief, until they both returned. What we didn't count on was that Kathy was older, wiser, and knew how to dish it out even better than us.

Mom came up the stairs with her hands on her hips in typical investigative fashion. "So, what do you boys have to say for yourselves?"

Wendell bragged at his success, "I'm guilty as sin!"

We were still giggling, and Mom warned, "Wipe those smirks off now, or I'll do it for you."

Before we could say anything, Kathy pointed and accused Wendell, "I was in there using the bathroom, and I caught him peeking through the crack in the door."

Holy cow! That's not what was happening, and she knew it. An accusation of moral perversity was a real game changer, and her lie instantly turned the tables. As a matter of fact, any allegation like that from the complementary gender in a situation like this was, pretty much, an immediate indictment of guilt.

Wendell was thunderstruck and objected, "I did not! That's not what I was doing!"

I tried to step in and explain what we'd really done, but it was too late. The gavel had fallen, and the verdict was already cast.

He got it good right there in the hallway, but the problem was that I couldn't stop laughing over the whole situation.

Wendell's idea was pretty dang cool, yet the way the situation had backfired was now totally hysterical.

Mom was enraged when she heard me laughing at my little brother's predicament. She looked over at me, and I dreaded what I heard, "Oh, so you think this is amusing, young man?" She grabbed my arm, yanked me close, and began whipping my butt too! With each whap, she said in staccato, "This – is - not – funny, - young – man!" Wendell was still crying from his spanking, but then began smiling and chuckling at me getting it, so Mom grabbed him once more and with the same rhythm in perfect tempo with the swing of her arm, she announced, "You – wait – till – your – father – gets – home!" Wendell was back to his tears again, and I was doing everything possible to maintain a straight face.

Boy, oh boy, was Mom ever pissed; especially in light of the weight of such a disturbing crime!

She hollered, "I thought your father and I raised you differently than that!"

That night, Dad gave us this huge lecture. "I know your Mom gave it to you both good this afternoon, so I'm not gonna' let you have it. But, if I ever hear about anything like this again..." He left the rest up to our imaginations which were wild and frightening.

Wendell and I probably fibbed several times every day, but Kathy lied so infrequently that Mom and Dad usually sided with her. She was smarter and knew just how to prove it; a Martin tried and true!

Axiom Sixteen
Endure hardship and celebrate survival.

Prankish antics continued right into our adulthood, and part of it was due to the conditioning stories we'd heard from our parents. If one of my uncles was visiting Dad and they went into a store, everyone knew they could never dare let the other guy out of sight.

My Dad had gone shopping with Uncle Mark. As they drove to the department story, Dad asked, "Hey Mark. I'm freezing. Can I borrow your Jacket? I just can't seem to get warm."

"Sure, Ralph. Here you go."

He took it off and passed it to my Dad, who wore it around the store for 15 minutes and did some jumping jacks like he was trying to warm up before giving it back.

"I'm good now. Thanks, Mark!"

"Sure, Ralph. Any time!"

The next thing my uncle knew was that his brother was nowhere to be found.

The store manager approached and asked, "Excuse me, sir, I couldn't happen but notice that you've got one of our silk ties in your jacket pocket that hasn't yet been paid for."

Uncle Mark said, "It suddenly hit me, what Ralph had been up to. I knew there was no way out of this, and so, I ended up paying for the tie. The worst part was going out of the store and finding that my brother had already gone home with my car! That dang Ralph had stolen the keys out of my jacket pocket!"

Our Moms would shake their heads, roll their eyes, and laugh till they cried at the mischief and trouble our uncles repeatedly caused one another. I think we understood our achievements as high-quality family entertainment. We, cousins, heard the stories and faced the challenge of outdoing our parents.

Axiom Seventeen
Whatever your talent, strive to be the best.

Wendell was very good at lacrosse and soccer. He could run, jump, spin, and maintain control of the ball. For a junior high school aged kid, he was truly amazing. In fact, he was probably the first guy in our clan who'd ever demonstrated talent in a skill that was legal and had the potential to be profitable.

Wendell could be charging downfield, full speed, straight toward an opponent and work a trick move that not only appeared to defy all the reasonable laws of physics, but moreover, would fool the perception of his challengers and allow him to repeatedly score. Imagine Wendell proficiently fielding the ball down field. At the last second, before colliding with a fast approaching adversary, he'd step in front of the ball with one foot, catch it up between his ankles, jump, and fling it in the air from behind. The ball would lob forward over their heads. By the time it landed behind his opponent, Wendell's agility and small size allowed him to dodge around, recover the ball, and make the goal. If there was ever a miracle play, Wendell had invented it. It really didn't matter if 6 players were converging on him all at once. In three seconds, he and the ball were already on the other side. By the time the opponents slowed, reversed direction, and began charging after him, it was too late. He'd outmaneuver much larger players and score more points than any of his teammates.

Uncle Tobias was stationed near Checkpoint Charlie at the Berlin Wall in Germany after the war. He'd married Aunt Frieda and stayed over there in her family's village of Schönholz.

When I was in about 7th grade, he saw a super-8 movie of Wendell playing soccer, which led to an offer to Mom and Dad that ended up being too difficult to refuse.

"Listen, Ralph and Elizabeth, Wendell's skill and talent with that ball is unbelievable! Nobody would think his moves were possible. We watch fútbol every Saturday in the Deutschland, and I'm telling you, with the right training, your boy has a future as a professional soccer player."

Our parents wanted the best for us kids and worked hard to provide all they could; however, we were only a blue-collar family with barely enough dough to keep food on the table. Mom and Dad had a strong desire for us kids to improve our legacy and worked round the clock at any endeavor possible to earn money. Nevertheless, they just couldn't get a break.

Uncle Tobias did his best to convince them, "You could use the educational trust, set up by my automotive firm, and Wendell could join Frieda and I to study at one of the famous sportschules. This could change his entire future."

Mom and Dad talked to Wendell about the opportunity, but he wavered about his own desire. On the one hand, he wanted to go. The offer and finances were a dream come true. On the other hand, he had an enormous fear of failure. Wendell felt as if he made the decision to go and something were to have happened, he'd fail and could never live with himself again. I never knew what in the heck was wrong with him, but it was definitely serious!

Nevertheless, after weeks of Uncle Tobias calling, encouraging, and negotiating with my little brother about the matter, Wendell finally was convinced to go for it. I'm not sure what they discussed or how they struck the deal, but the whole thing was a much bigger and required more effort than I ever would have imagined. Dang it all anyway! I'd have jumped at that kind of opportunity in a heartbeat without ever looking back! But then again, Mr. Washington always reflected critically, "Levi, your feet always arrive on the doorstep of trouble a minute or two before your brains!" I knew that he meant well, and I'd usually agree after the paddlings I received in his office.

Axiom Eighteen
Love your neighbor.

Try as they may, each working several different jobs, Mom and Dad could never seem to get ahead. Someone in our families was always in need, and a couple times they'd put up bail money for our cousins. It's just how things rolled. My parents seldom said "No." Mom would discover a kid on our street without shoes and the boy or girl would often find a pair miraculously appearing on the doorstep. Our dinner table was always jammed with neighborhood youth who Mom suspected weren't being well fed. Pastor James never went without a new suit each Christmas, although he never knew the source of his blessing. They seemed to cherish making the annual arrangements to surprise him more than they would have enjoyed a vacation.

I was privy to the knowledge only because of my secret hallway listening post outside our bedroom door. On a regular basis, I'd hide there and catch up on household management issues over their regular dining room or front porch coffee dates. My parents didn't have to travel the world to find peace or satisfaction. Our home or the lake my uncle lived near were always their favorite highly affordable destinations.

36

The only reason Wendell and Kathy never turned me in for listening in on their conversations was my agreement to keep them both filled in on the news. I'd heard Mom tell Aunt Jenny once, as they sat at the dining room table discussing an upcoming wedding, "Ralph's suit still looks pretty good." In reality, it was an antique, old enough to have gone in and out of style twice. Yet, Mom and Dad were more about function than fashion. Living simply allowed them to squeeze pennies and dollars from the meager budget in order to help others.

After Mr. Buller next door had a stroke and was forced to use a wheelchair, Dad used his vacation allowance he'd saved for a fishing trip, instead, to build the neighbors a ramp going from the driveway up to their front door. On dark, snowy mornings before going to work, Dad, Wendell, and I got up early to shovel and salt their drive and walkway.

Mom wore the only pair of sandals she had through that whole winter, smiling politely at those who looked at her feet questioningly and thought better of her.

Mrs. Buller commented, "Why, Elizabeth, your feet must be freezing!"

Mom bragged, "I love these sandals so much Jessica; I just can't bear to wear anything else."

I alone knew that they were the only shoes Mom owned. She happily endured the cold, knowing that the rest of us were better taken care of. Dad needed what few warmer clothes she could find and afford at the thrift store, so she said, because he worked outside through the winter.

My parents were awesome providers for us kids and the hood. They always cared more for everyone else around them than they did for themselves.

Sadly, that spring, "Mr. Buller, passed into the loving arms of the Almighty." That's how Pastor James had put it. After that tragic loss, Mom made certain that Jessica Buller was a constant guest in our home with a regular place setting at our table. If you knew my parents, you understood that our neighbors were the same as kin. Neither denomination, political affiliation, color, nor race mattered. It seemed as if one of Mom and Dad's favorite sayings was, "It's not about the skin, it's all about kin!" I heard Mom comment a few times, "Putting a smile on another person's face in this life with a good meal is real evidence that the Lord's happiness is shining through them." Boy, did she ever work hard to take care of everyone she could, no matter what it cost!

It wouldn't be too many years later that I'd begin amassing a fortune and Dad would begin receiving unexpected bonuses. For my own part, I became trapped in a world where I'd never be able to spend most of the cash. The American Dream eluded me. Eventually, we'll get to all of that.

Axiom Nineteen
Remain persistent.

Because of Uncle Tobias' and Aunt Frieda's generosity, the summer before my freshman year, Wendell attended a sports camp in Germany. Although they'd been negotiating with my younger brother and twisting my parents' arms to let him go to the Deutschland, in the end, it was due to a series of events and a fist fight that Wendell disappeared from our lives across the lake. It's a long story to be told later on. Despite the fact that my parents had never known personally what a savings account was, because of the educational trust funded by Uncle Tobias' company, my brother would receive the best academic and athletic training, giving him the potential to live on as a soccer star.

Mom and Dad often said, "By hook or crook, you kids will be the first of the Martins to attend college." They bragged, "Kathy will either become a teacher or a nurse." Their vision for our future wellbeing, however unlikely it seemed due to their limited resources, was all that they hoped for. They wanted their children to become people of importance with the potential to escape the seemingly perpetual, hopeless destiny of rural poverty.

Axiom Twenty
Reflect and become someone new,
preferably someone generous and admirable.

The strong sense of shame I felt in social studies class when Mr. Cline's map was pulled down also signified a small turning point in my life. After 8th grade, I'd spent some time in Germany where it was a far more serious world. This had changed me. I carried some secrets and never realized how heavy they'd weigh upon me.

During my senior year at Bodega High, I wavered back and forth between living as Mr. Serious and Mr. Fun-loving Levi. Admittedly, the caper involving the map wasn't one of my finer moments. The naïve idealism within me struggled against the harsh, factual, rationalism that was so characteristic of Uncle Tobias' world. I saw myself evolving into adulthood and didn't always like who I'd been, but at the same time, I struggled to let go of the carefree life that could be afforded in the cloistered recesses of a town like Bodega. The passionate love of freedom held its grip on me, but inwardly, a war waged in my psyche. At that age, sometimes I thought I was smart enough to rule the world. Life still had some tough lessons that would bring me up to speed with reality.

I lamented more than once, "How could I have done something so maliciously evil to Mr. Cline?" He was such an awesome teacher. The bitter taste of regret helped me to see what an idiot I'd been, seasoning my future with positive changes. In a world of fools, perhaps there was even hope for me.

Mom and Dad were tremendously proud of us boys. For a while in the summer between my junior and senior years, things looked bad for my father. He suffered a series of health problems, and doctors thought he wasn't going to pull out of it. Eventually, with Mom's constant care, he recovered. Due to his illness, Kathy got some early training nursing Dad back to health.

When Dad was back on his feet, he worked night and day to save money for Kathy's schooling, and she did the same as well. None of us were freeloaders. In those days, "student loans" didn't exist. Lenders meted out funds only to those who could prove ownership of property as collateral. Then, a miracle happened. A check came in the mail, made payable to a medical college that would cover every penny of my sister's education; taking her all the way to becoming a doctor if that's what she chose.

Immediately, Dad got on the phone to his brother across the lake in the Deutschland at more than a dollar per minute, "Tobias, this isn't going to do! Just because you've done better than the rest of us, doesn't mean we can accept your charity.

Elizabeth, Kathy, and I are all working hard and we're going to figure this thing out for ourselves!"

Dad took tremendous pride in providing for his family.

"I promise you, Ralph, I don't have any idea what you're talking about."

"Look, you and Frieda were kind with getting Wendell into that fancy German sports gymnasium, and Elizabeth and I are really grateful you love us so much to do that. But, hear me now, you know damn well what I'm talking about with Kathy! You're the only one who'd pull a stunt like this!"

Frieda got on the other line, "Ralph, you have to believe your brother. I'm telling you the truth. We don't know anything at all about what's going on with Kathy, except that she's saving for her nursing program. The only thing we've done to help is to send her $100 last Christmas and this year on her birthday."

Their argument cost Dad nearly $60 on the phone bill, until my parents were completely convinced that neither Tobias, Frieda, nor his educational trust had anything to do with the mysterious arrival of an anonymous check. They never knew where the money had come from. Kathy had applied and was pre-enrolled, pending financial arrangements. Mom and Dad finally forwarded the check on to the school, and that was that. My sister was on her way to a bright future.

Several weeks later, my parents were convinced they'd discovered the source of the finances. I heard them talking in hushed tones and stopped at my listening post in the hall.

"Darling. I figured it out!"

"What honey?"

"Kathy's college money."

"Yeah? Where did it come from?"

"I'll bet that Jessica Buller had a life insurance policy for George, and she's paid Kathy's way."

"Well, honey, that would sure make sense. Ya' know that kind of cash just doesn't appear out of thin air. I suppose you may be right. Should we talk to her about it?"

Mom thought for a minute.

"Nope. If Jessica wanted to keep it a secret, then that's that. We'll just have to be humble and grateful."

The Martins shared a strong sense of pride over their ability to figure things out. Nevertheless, Mom was blissfully mistaken.

Axiom Twenty-One
Whatever it takes, go to college.

Between Dad being deathly ill, then regaining his health, the miraculous provision for Kathy's education, and Mom getting me ready for college, there was a constant whirlwind of ongoing change for all my senior year. Wendell would shortly graduate from the Sportschule Geisbach Gymnasium, in the Rhein-Seig district of North Rhine Westphalia, and luckily, my parents had gotten to fly over and visit him a several times over the last few years. The trust covered airfare. He and I weren't much for writing letters and had fallen out of touch. Wendell and I didn't get to talk much, but we chatted on the phone during the holidays.

At soccer, he'd become even faster, more agile, and well-practiced. He could whip any player's butt and was destined for great things.

I visited once, and surprisingly, he told me how grateful he was to the Almighty. He explained emphatically, "If I couldn't become a soccer star, I wouldn't want to live!"

Wendell's life had always been characterized by extremes, but his comment was beyond what I considered to be normal. Mom and Dad had raised us to passionately pursue what and who we loved. Although none of us knew it would be so short lived, I was happy to see his dream coming true.

For my own part, it had been decided that I'd pursue earth sciences and geology. It took some serious arm-twisting, but Dad finally relented at Uncle Tobias' and Aunt Frieda's insistence that he should allow them to pay for the rest of my education.

He pleaded, "Ralph and Elizabeth, we've done so much for Wendell, that you have to let us make this equal with Levi!" Since keeping things fair was also a strong family value, finally, my parents agreed. They insisted though that they'd take care of my pocket money for incidentals.

That summer we packed all my gear into our 20+-year-old white station wagon and drove nearly nonstop to Delphi College in Narrows Creek, New York. I'd intended to explore every club and student interest and secured a volunteer position as an assistant editor of the school paper. Several guys and gals attended an orientation meeting to learn more. I had hoped to be accepted on to the paper's staff, and out of all those gathered, I'd gotten the lucky break. But then, unexpectedly, there was a change.

It confused and flustered my parents a little, but a week or so later, it was decided that I'd switch to the State University of New York College at New Paltz; several hours further away. I explained that it cost less money and they offered a better geological engineering degree.

After they called Tobias and were assured that he'd get a refund from Delphi, they quit worrying about any of it.

Axiom Twenty-Two
Work to become a leader,
lest you end up taking orders from someone less educated.

When I was settled in, I discovered the excitement of college life and was amazed at all the groups, clubs, and gatherings. I visited them all. My greatest hope was to get into a fraternity. The movie, "Animal House," had come out recently, and those guys looked like they were definitely having a blast. I wanted to get my own fair share of the fun.

Because I had almost become a volunteer editor for the Delphi Observer, the school began forwarding issues of their campus newspaper to my new address. This reminded me to check out the New Paltz classifieds to find even more local events and meetings. I joined the outing, photography, and frisbee golf clubs. I checked out every crazy religious and new age gathering on and off the campus. I even tried tennis, golf, and bowling. A fun-loving guy like me was eventually destined for something they called, "academic probation." But, that didn't happen until my second semester.

My favorite campus organization was the New Paltz Outing Club. The village is situated in the valley looking up at the impressive granite Shawangunk Ridge. It's renowned as the best place for rock climbing in the northeastern United States.

My skills in chimneying between outcroppings caught the

attention of the outing club leaders.

For those who may not be familiar with the term, "chimneying," it is a climbing skill used to ascend or descend narrow channels between vertical walls. By applying opposing force to flanking surfaces using your back, arms, legs, hands, and feet, the rigidity of the pressure maintained against parallel surfaces suspends your body, allowing you to hold a position or to gradually move side to side, upward, or downward. This was a special talent in which I excelled, and it impressed the directors of the New Paltz Outing Club.

Whereas most people could chimney by pressuring their back against a surface pushing off another with their hands and feet, I had the proper weight, balance, core strength and agility to support my body horizontally; feet touching one surface and hands stretched across to the other. I could brace my body flat and level between two vertical surfaces and remain still for about 10 minutes straight. Furthermore, under ideal conditions, I could walk straight upward or downward facing the sky or the ground.

One of the club leaders watched me demonstrate the move up in the, "Gunks," as the cliffs and mountains were affectionately labeled, and he said, "Hey wait. Hold it right there."

I was suspended about 6' off the ground. He stood beneath me reaching up with his fingertip, looking as if he were supporting me, while someone took our picture.

Showing off my skill, I worked my way up about 20' higher and then back down between two adjacent, vertical slabs of granite.

"Where did you learn that, Levi? Most of us would've used ropes to make that kind of ascent."

On the same trip, we'd done some repelling, and I'd shown the guys a whole new set of stronger knots that were faster to tie.

"We're pretty impressed, Levi."

"I've been climbing 10 years and I've never heard of the 'clove hitch,' a 'bow line,' or the 'sheet bend.' How about coming out next weekend for our final gathering of the year and making a demonstration. I think we're in agreement that you deserve consideration as a new leader in the club."

To say the least, I was stoked! Those hot summer days of practice in the ropes course as a junior high schooler in Base Camp were about to pay off handsomely! Additionally, I planned to throw in 40 minutes of compass work and to demonstrate using a magnifying glass to start a fire.

"Adara, my sweet friend, you'll soon be unleashed once again."

Axiom Twenty-Three
The person who needs the deal more always loses in the negotiations.

Desperation is leverageable, and some SUNY professors bartered with students of impoverished academic status to set up and serve at department meetings. When they offered us extra points on the next exam in exchange for our help, our poor grades didn't leave us with much of a choice.

"Hey, Levi, I've got a deal you can't refuse. I need help Saturday for a staff luncheon. We're demonstrating the new electron microscope to the professors at the school, and I wonder if you could set up the gymnasium with tables and chairs. On Friday afternoon and evening, I also need someone to prepare the vegetable trays, pick up condiments, and to lay out the plastic tablecloths. If it all looks perfect for our meeting, I'm willing to add ten extra points to your next exam grade."

Doctor Adler was the department head as well as my paleontology professor. He knew he had me because of my failing grades, and I was ticked! This meant I wouldn't be confirmed Saturday as a trip leader in the New Paltz Outing Club. DANG!

"Certainly, Dr. Adler. I'd love to help."

I cheerfully agreed but harbored resentment deep inside. As fate would have it, my professor's leverage forced me to cancel the momentous engagement on the Shawangunk Ridge. Knowing I'd have to wait until the following spring for another opportunity, I stewed about it until my anger hardened into a grudge. Eventually, it became a full-fledged ax to grind.

Of course, if I'd taken notes in class, read the textbook, and had done my homework, things probably would've been different. At that point in my life, however, it was easier to blame others than to take responsibility for my own destiny.

Dr. Adler was sly and the way he used me continued to tick me off. Rumor had it that once he'd roped a guy into cutting his lawn for the semester in exchange for special tutoring. The student ended up with an "A." Something sounded fishy about the whole deal.

Quite often, I was also suckered into cleaning the paleontology lab, sorting, packing, and moving trays of fossils back into storage, just to receive five measly points on the next quiz.

Onlookers at staff luncheons could easily identify the

students who were worse off grade-wise by their frequent indentured servitude. By early October, I'd peeled carrots and chopped vegetables on several occasions in order to raise my class average from an "F" to a "D."

Axiom Twenty-Four
There is often more than one way to interpret communication. Seek what is less than obvious.

One collegiate gathering I attended was different from all the rest and changed the course of my future. It was an advertisement on a bulletin board that led me to the event. The sign read:

New at New Paltz? Love adventure?
Join us Friday evening for food, friends, and fun!

The evening was unusual and enjoyable, that is, if you thought behaving goofy was fun. Everyone was acting silly except for the quiet man with graying hair who reclined in an easy chair over by the corner. He smoked a pipe and watched casually, almost seeming not to care what was happening around him. The fragrance of cherry tobacco wafted through the air. The windows were open, and it was a beautiful, breezy, September evening.

Most of us were first-year students. As newbies, we shared the common quality of uncertainty about our new surroundings. We were vulnerable and open to new ideas. The event was an opportunity for exposure to different perspectives and cultural growth. Acting ridiculous came easy, because we were all in the same boat. Few of us seemed to know anyone else at the gathering, and we had nothing to lose.

Axiom Twenty-Five
Props and artifacts can deceive.
Beware of how you interpret the world around you.

It was evident that the man in the chair owned the house. Several pictures of him with those who were obviously also his family adorned the walls. I noticed in a few photos that he had a cute daughter, although, she was probably too old for me. She stood in front of a brownstone between her parents. Her father hugged her and she looked up at him admiringly. His wife smiled sweetly. The photos must have been taken in New York City or at other locations outside of the quaint little village that was home to the State University of New York College.

An ornately framed plaque with a fancy laminated certificate was proudly displayed on the wall for "Dr. Elias Jefferson." It was a Ph.D. in something I don't recall from Columbia University. I surmised that he must have been a professor here at the school.

When folks asked where you were going to college, you most often simply replied using the acronym and location: "SUNY at New Paltz."

Back then, it was a cool little hippy town stuck in the 60s. Tie-dyed dresses and t-shirts hung outside the shop doors on Main Street. There was a guy dressed a lot like Mr. Bojangles, who frequented the steps of several establishments along the way. More than once, his frail looking frame caught my attention. I identified with him because, like me, he usually had a bandana hanging out of his pocket. He often loitered with a friendly smile and fit right in with the backdrop of the boutiques.

At night, the village became a boozing college town. The amazing aroma of NY style pizza drifted outside those establishments. Your mouth watered whenever you walked by! Although I was from California, I learned to eat the slices folded in half like a New Yorker. I regretted not having saved more cash from my summer job just for that indescribable meal. Little did I know, it wouldn't be long before I'd have all the pizza, calzones, and burgers my heart desired.

Axiom Twenty-Six
At parties, people tend to lower their guard.
Never lower your guard anywhere!

Tonight was different than most other Fridays. After Bible study, I'd often be found down at Brandus shooting pool. Instead, I enjoyed hospitality in a real person's home named "Elias Jefferson." I wasn't convinced about the advertised "adventure" part of the deal, but I assumed this had to do with bobbing for apples that was about to begin shortly in the backyard.

The "Master of Ceremonies" at the event was nicknamed "M.C. Josef." He gave the instructions, "Stick out your tongue and touch your nose."

Now, I watched all these guys and chicks sticking their tongues out and reaching elusively for their noses. It was kind of bizarre. I caught Josef's eye and stuck out my tongue and touched my nose with my right index finger. He smiled, nodded, and then candidly made a mark on his roster. I wondered incredulously, "Did he just write down what I did?"

Later, I casually walked by to look at his clipboard, but he held it close to his chest as I passed. I pretended not to notice, just like Dr. Jefferson who also seemed to be pretending not to observe who was doing what.

I pointed out a particularly funny looking tongue contortionist by the wall to a girl standing next to me. We laughed. I used the diversion to glance back at the observant man in the corner. "Mr. Gray Hair in the Chair" was sharp as an eagle paying attention to everyone in the room at once. Was he paranoid about someone stealing his degree from the wall or his books from the shelves? He seemed to be simultaneously listening in on every conversation in the room.

I recall considering the oddity that this guy would make a good spy in an action adventure. He was benevolent, sharp, calculated, and innocent looking. Why did I have this impression of the man? The thought came and went with the passing of the fall breeze. I'd later recall having had that intuition several months later in a drastically altered set of circumstances, as he threateningly loaded a .45 caliber Colt and held me captive.

Axiom Twenty-Seven
If there are no explicit rules, make your own.
It's safer to ask forgiveness than permission.

We went outside to bob for apples, and Josef commented, "You all know the rules and need to abide by them!" He was polite but sounded a little too serious for me.

The galvanized barrels in which the beautiful, round, red pieces of Edenic fruit were floating, allowed enough room for a dozen participants to partake in the frivolity at once. I decided to wait for the second round of contestants, but the sight of those ripe, delicious apples made me hungry! Before they were all covered with breath mint laden slobber, at the risk of breaking the rules, I passed by, reached in fast, and grabbed one to eat.

I shook the water off my hand and figured that since the M.C. hadn't actually stated any explicit regulations for the game, I could make my own. Josef noticed, turned aside, and marked something down. It was the second time I saw him do that and it was weirding me out. Had he been keeping a scorecard on each of us all night?

So, then, we all lined up with our feet tight against a wall. This time, Josef explained the single rule that our shoes had to remain touching the baseboard. Then, he littered the ground in front of each of us with several dollars. He said that if we could pick up any of the bills, they were ours to keep. In moments, each of us discovered the problem. While maintaining this stance, it was impossible to reach down to the floor without falling over.

I had an idea. I was next to a corner, and there was a skinny chick next to me. I glanced at her fast and whispered, "Do you want to make five bucks?" She smiled and nodded inquisitively. I suggested, "I think we can do this if we work together." I reached over and grabbed her belt and held it to the wall. Because her waist was pinned back, she proved to be the only one in the room who could double over to reach the ground.

After grabbing several dollars off the floor, she counted out five singles for herself and handed me the remaining sixth bill.

I looked oddly at her like I'd been cheated and said, "What's up with that?"

She cleverly replied, "You made the deal, not me. A $5 deal is a $5 deal!"

Then, I saw Josef and Dr. Jefferson staring at each other and back at us like we'd broken the rules.

I shrugged at them and said, "You never said we couldn't help one another. Is there a law against teamwork or the 'Golden Rule?'"

They both nodded and smiled. Josef wrote something else down.

After the party, I asked the girl if she was from California.

"Nope. I'm from Kankakee, Illinois."

There was something oddly familiar about her.

I asked further, "Did you ever visit Bodega or the west coast?"

"No."

Hmmm. Did you ever have the strange feeling you'd met someone previously, but couldn't put your finger on precisely where?

What I should have asked was, "Did you ever attend Delphi College?"

Axiom Twenty-Eight
When you're being watched, perform well.
Life is an audition.

So, we played all these strange mind-bending games the entire evening and ended with an odd one. Josef handed out those small half pencils with no eraser and some scraps of paper and asked, "If your friend was feeling ill, how could you make her feel better?" He further instructed, "Go ahead and write your answer."

Well, dog-gone-it-all-anyway! You would've thought we were a gathering of medical students! A few of these folks had to get several sheets to elucidate what they might do. One girl explained employment of the Heimlich Maneuver. I questioned myself with alarm, "Isn't that the procedure to help someone who's choking?" I made a mental note to never become her friend! Some just looked really perplexed. The guy next to me was sentimental and straight to the point. He wrote, "I'd tell my comrade an encouraging story."

The $5 girl was catching on to the mind games and she wrote, "your answer."

I gave it another moment's thought and scribbled the word "better" on the scrap of paper. I caught Josef's eye, flashed up my response so he could read it and then rubbed it with my finger. I told him, *"This is how you make someone feel 'better!'"* He smiled, shook his head and got busy with his pen once more. If he was, in fact, keeping score, then I was doing pretty darn good.

So, I began to wonder, "Is this some sort of test or rite of passage leading into a fraternity?" By the time the party broke up at 10:00, I'd become convinced this was the case. I wondered which one and why those organizations all had Greek letters for names. For certain, based upon my skilled performance, they'd invite me to join soon.

I wandered downtown to see if the pool table at Brandus was still accessible. Later, it struck me oddly to think that nobody had ever mentioned the name of the group that sponsored the gathering.

Axiom Twenty-Nine
Things aren't always as they appear.

For my own part, I assumed that Dr. Jefferson must have been a SUNY professor, and that he owned the quaint house where the gathering took place. It was plainly obvious that he was a graduate of Columbia University. But, as it turned out, none of these pieces of information proved to be factual. Was the girl in the photo standing with him in front of the brownstone really his daughter? No. It was a staged picture designed to leave its viewer with a certain kind of impression of the party host.

Everyone who attended the gathering and viewed these props left committed to the notion that Elias Jefferson was a kindhearted family man; a professor and a wise person any of us would trust. In a few months, I'd discover that he was one of the most ruthless men alive.

We have a natural tendency to unquestioningly assimilate what we see or hear and regard things as true. Because of this, with careful planning, settings can be staged to leave certain impressions in the minds of others. The intellectual facets that form into ideas, accumulate subconsciously. They get put together subliminally, often becoming regarded as certainties which further guide our judgment and decisions. IPM existed in an artificial world. Every aspect of how they operated was set up to gain control of peoples' thoughts. Because of this, eventually, they could control others' actions.

Axiom Thirty
Assumptions can lead to danger.
Reflect on what you think is true and be safe.

We interpret sights and sounds in the world around us, often assigning meaning to events and information which may or may not be valid. Is the lady pushing a cart at the shopping center there to shop? Does the man on the utility pole outside work for the phone company?

Imagine the scenario where we see a passerby on the sidewalk who waves at our neighbor, Jim. The stranger smiles broadly and addresses him, "Hey, Jim, how about that 49ers game last night?"

The amiable attitude and friendly gesture we observe influences us. We unquestioningly conclude that the pedestrian must be a friend of our neighbor. He might be trustworthy.

By degree, with the example above, we tend to make progressive gradual assumptions that lump themselves together into erroneous conclusions. *Jim must be friends with that guy. They both like football. Jim has a certain degree of trust for that man. I think he must be a good person. I can probably trust him too.* Ideas, which are taken for granted, become embedded within our minds and grow. These become stepping stones, allowing others pathways into our worlds and building blocks upon which false notions find firm foundations.

Because individuals don't learn to identify and call assumptions into question, these develop into cerebral fulcrums, allowing the unsuspecting to be leveraged, deceived, and victimized. Things that we think are true, but are not, can be used to manipulate our thoughts, choices, and actions. Oftentimes, the naïve proceed casually through life, basing decisions on a growing myriad of blind suppositions. They innocently become easy prey.

Axiom Thirty-One
We live in a sinister world. Beware!

IPM instructed participants how to turn those around them into easy prey. We studied the motivations, fears, and secrets of our targets, until we harnessed power and control. Taking advantage of their character flaws, guilt, secrets, and intellectual frailties, we formed decisive strategies and honed these into tools of terror.

We gained the means to build realms of false security, allowing us to later plant imaginary threats in the psyches of our victims. As they were gradually led to place trust in facades, we assumed power. Then, we pushed them outside of their comfort zones and assaulted them with shocking, frightening, threats that would precipitate reactionary attitudes and decisions. When you attain domination over a target's mind, you control his assertions of power, relationships, assets, and his destiny. We watched as well-orchestrated programs caused seemingly invincible empires to crumble. Therein, we altered the courses of many lives and changed the future.

My first two weeks of college went by before I met up with Josef again. He was at the entry stairs to the dining hall. I said, "Hey, 'Master of Ceremonies!' Waiting for someone?"

He replied, "Hi, Levi. No, well, she probably stood me up."

I was full of myself and thought, "Then she's probably a smart girl!" I nodded and motioned for him to join me upstairs.

"So, what were all those games about at that party, and what were you writing down?" I was surprised that he seemed to be honest with me after his cloak and dagger actions at the gathering.

"It was a challenge to find students who think outside-the-box."

"Why? Was that the rite of initiation for a frat house?"

I felt proud of my deductive abilities, when Josef responded, "You're sure good at figuring things out, Levi."

"Yes! I knew it!" Not that it would've made any difference, but I asked, "Which fraternity?"

Josef said, "I guess you'll just have to wait and see."

He knew how to work my curiosity.

"We'll see how it goes, and maybe I can explain more later. For now, let's just see what you do with some opportunities we give you. Our openings are limited in number, so we have to remain choosy."

"Dang!" I hated waiting, especially for something like this that I'd been hoping for.

"Well, Josef, can you at least tell me how I did at the party?"

He grinned and replied in a sassy tone, "Pretty darn good for a guy who breaks the rules and makes up his own along the way!"

I smiled back, but also objected, "Are you calling me a 'cheater?'"

"No, you didn't cheat, but you ignored some conventions."

"Wha-da-ya' mean? Ya' know I'm only a freshman, so I'm not used to four-syllable words!"

He began to sound out, "con-ven..."

I interrupted and pointed at him accusingly with a smirk. "Gotcha!"

I knew he was about to correct the fact that the term had only three syllables.

He remarked, "You're just full of surprises, Mr. Martin!"

Actually, I was just full of nonsense.

Axiom Thirty-Two
Beware of seeming chess masters.
Some use unfair advantages.

A few days later, Josef showed up for dinner at his usual table carrying a chessboard. I admitted that I wasn't very talented at the game. Nevertheless, he asked if I'd endure a few rounds to help him write a research paper regarding probabilities in the use of pawns. This sounded like a joke, but I agreed. We played six games and he whooped my butt every single time! Most chess players remain silent during the competition, but Josef was like the combination of vocal sports announcer and interviewer for the National Chess Federation.

Near the end of my slaughter, in the last challenge, Josef recited the number of times in each game I'd used my pawn; either to block or as an aggressor. He went on to explain something about why I had so easily lost my queen in three of the matches. Then, he astutely provided the mathematical statistics for my moves without having written anything down the whole time we played. I figured he had an I.Q. of a million or more and a videographic memory!

"Holy cow, Josef, you probably shouldn't be writing a paper about all this. I think you ought to be teaching the class!"

"That's kind of you, Levi, but don't change the subject. I wanted to point out that in the second game, on your third move, you were aggressing toward my knight. This altered the likelihood of a win, because the decision exposed your queen."

I interrupted, "Wait a minute!" I reached over and tipped the beret he wore up off his head.

He objected, "What are you doing, Levi?"

"Just checking to see if you have pointy ears and if you're Vulcan."

Need I mention that just like the character we've all seen in the movies, he wasn't even slightly amused.

Josef continued to ramble on for 15 minutes about that same pawn. An hour later, he'd only finished discussing our 4th game. He'd memorized every move I'd taken and the rationale behind my decision to use the chess piece.

"Josef! How can you possibly recite all this and even detail my very own thought processes on every single play? This is too much to believe. Are you one of those guys who can also recite all the presidents of the United States?" He didn't answer. At the end of decoding each of my pawn moves in the 4th game, I finally had to interrupt him again.

"Look, man, you're simply astounding! I have to beg for mercy and stop, now though, because it's giving me a headache thinking back through every game like this. I hope what we've already accomplished will help you complete your thesis."

He really was like something from another planet. Later, I found out that the project had nothing to do with a college course or writing a paper.

Axiom Thirty-Three
There are different methods of thinking fast.

Have you seen the movie "Limitless" or the "Jason Bourne" series? The commonality of those scripts that's accurate is the actual existence of the kind of mind-altering medicine they portrayed. The government didn't just experiment with lysergic acid diethylamide (LSD) in the 60s, they kept testing all kinds of chemicals in people's brains. They also came up with a few formulas that can make a person think fast – very, very fast!

Certain substances can cause the mind to process information at astounding rates of speed, having the perceptive effect of slowing time down. The user manages so much information in any given moment that it seems as if the world and people are moving in slow motion around him. In situations of great stress when someone's life depends upon quick thinking, the meds seemingly provided extra time to figure out a variety of different solutions to eliminate threats.

The 2009 Warner Bros. rendition of Sherlock Holmes, starring Robert Downey Jr., provides a cinema graphic example that portrayed this kind of speed of light perception (although this was simply the Holmes character's natural ability). In the fighting ring, between punches, Holmes viewed the event almost as if he could see into the future. He had the talent to predict the actions of his competitor and could plan the next half dozen moves necessary to knock out his opponent.

I didn't learn about this medication until a year or so after my initial involvement with IPM. There's lots to say about this, but I'll wait until I get to those stories. Suffice to say, Josef hadn't naturally been simultaneously a genius chess champion, professional commentator, and statistician all on his own!

I should mention that in the world of espionage, the game of chess became metaphoric of the method allowing for a spy's enduring existence. In order to stay alive, you had to always keep track of what any person knew about you. It was necessary in order to anticipate their thinking and predict their actions. In many instances, you had to plant an idea in their minds about your intentions to manipulate a response or set up an alibi. Trickery of this sort could give you a necessary advantage over your coworker or adversary; who sometimes were one and the same.

Axiom Thirty-Four

Learning theorists with limited perception have accepted that I.Q. can't be improved. Never listen to close-minded thinkers or you'll live within their dull confines. Your abilities are staggering!

"So," Josef asked, "Do you ever read Dominion Magazine?"

"My friend, Tim, had a subscription in high school, and it always had cool articles."

"Did you see the recent issue with the purported 'World's Most Exacting I.Q. Test?'"

"Yes, did you write that?" He ignored my question, and so, I continued, "I think it was published in 1978."

Joseph asked, "Do you know anyone who took the test? Readers could send in their responses to the editors or someone who designed the exam to grade and analyze the results."

Conveniently, he had a photocopy for me to give it a whirl if I wanted.

"It's yours, but can you return it to me soon?"

I agreed, "Okay."

A week later I gave it back to him. Then, odd as it may seem, I didn't see or hear from Josef again for several years.

In the next couple of weeks, I wondered what happened. I never saw him at the cafeteria table where he always ate dinner. Did he get sick, leave school, or get raptured? After a while, it occurred to me that I might inquire about other students at the business office. They weren't helpful at all! So, I thought I'd drop by Dr. Jefferson's house. There was a real-estate sign in the front yard. "For Sale." I looked in the porch window, but the place was completely empty. I didn't give up but went to search the faculty tower. All that I could discover was that nobody had ever heard of "Dr. Elias Jefferson."

And so began what I eventually called "mind games" and my fateful involvement with IPM. Had I known that solving the mystery of Jefferson's identity was nearly going to cost my life at the hands of a foreign warlord in the next 90 days, I'd have walked away right then and there.

Axiom Thirty-Five
Beware of flattery combined with invitations from casual acquaintances.

Prior to finding the "For Sale" sign in Jefferson's front yard, I'd attended a second party at his home and met a new guy named "Jacob" who served as the M.C.

He approached and greeted me, "You must be 'Levi.' Welcome! Dr. Jefferson mentioned that you came up with some creative ways of playing our games last time. He remarked that you were 'clever and resourceful.' Josef described you in a word as being 'innovative.'"

"Oh, hi. Thanks!"

I wasn't sure how to respond and wondered how this stranger knew me by name when I'd just walked in the front door.

I played it cool, "Yeah, it was a fun evening," Then, I shifted gears, "Say, have you seen Josef recently?"

Jacob was quiet at first, but then he responded, "I think he left school. I haven't run into him for a while."

It was sort of an awkward moment, but I asked, "Did you ever play chess with him?"

Jacob smiled briefly, then said, "No, why do you ask?"

I said, "Oh, never mind." But then, because I was a Martin, and I knew he was holding out on me, I couldn't resist manipulating the guy's ignorance to have some fun. So, I went on, "He and I played a few games and I beat him pretty bad. I thought maybe he was avoiding me because I'd hurt his feelings."

Jacob's jaw dropped, betraying his disbelief, "You beat Josef at chess?" He paused, then he added, "More than once?"

"Well, actually it was six games. Before we began, Josef seemed confident in his abilities, and he was a good sport about all of it in the end. Do me a favor though, let's keep quiet about it. I don't want to upset him by making him think I was bragging about my victories; you know just in case he returns anytime soon."

It was odd because it was almost as if Jacob needed half a moment to recover, but then he continued matter-of-factly, "You must be quite talented to have beaten him. I've heard that he's pretty good. Were you in a chess club in high school?"

I lied a little more, "Na, well actually, my uncle plays chess for money and he's taught me a few strategies."

This new guy seemed to believe me, but he came off almost sounding in his tone as if he was miffed about my supposed victories. He continued with his greeting, except now, he lacked the same cheerful enthusiasm, "We're glad you've joined us once again, Levi. We hope that you have a good time. What's your major?"

"Geological engineering. As a kid, I was always intrigued by different minerals and crystals." I smiled and further responded, "So, what fraternity sponsors this meeting?"

"Well, we're not a formal organization on campus. Dr. Jefferson is just a local guy who enlisted Josef, myself, and others to help him gather information for a book he's writing on problem-solving."

I thought to myself, "DANG!" Things were just starting to look good for scoring entry into the frat house. Now those hopes were shattered. UGH! I was even more miffed that Josef had tricked me.

"Oh, then that's why Josef was keeping track of our responses on a clipboard last time?"

He replied in a more stern, inquisitive sort of way, "You noticed? Well, yes. Dr. Jefferson was impressed with the ways you navigated the evening and has invited you to help with future meetings. As he forges ahead in his research, he has a few fun and adventurous challenges to offer; that is, if you're up for them."

Jacob paused, looking at me with a faint smile. There was a challenge in his demeanor. He was setting me up, but at this age, I was too immature to recognize the dynamic of flattery followed by a daring request. Also, I was still caught off guard for the moment with the realization that my dream of this leading to significance as a frat brother had abruptly ended. Still, though, Jacob's compliments aroused a feeling of pride.

I plodded ahead into our discussion, not having the faintest clue of the trouble I was about to get myself into, "Really, like what?"

Once again, he became more animated, "Well, Levi, you know we challenge students with these absurd games at the parties?"

"Yes."

"Actually, those serve as a process of elimination. Dr. Jefferson is hoping to find the brightest students to focus on in certain chapters of his book."

My hope was renewed as I realized this might turn out better than the fraternity. However, if I'd actually had a clue at that point in my life, I'd have asked, "If he's looking for smart students, then why is he interested in me?" Ignorance is bliss.

Axiom Thirty-Six
Examine your motivations.
The desire for fame is dangerous.

"Really, you mean I could be famous?"

Jacob laughed, "Well, I suppose that's one way to look at it. Jefferson has two chapters that you might find interesting."

"Yeah? Tell me about them."

I was like a lemming, naively eager to jump to his peril.

"One has to do with escapes. Several situations will be set up wherein the person Dr. Jefferson chooses will have to get away by running, hiding, or otherwise eluding an actual pursuer."

"You mean someone is really going to chase us?" This sounded cool! "Well, I'm interested."

"Another section of the book has to do with maneuvering through a demanding situation. It's more of an intellectual kind of predicament. A set of unusual circumstances will be arranged, which will test the contender's wit, negotiating skills, and thinking abilities. Essentially, you'd have to figure out the means to turn around a disadvantage in which you found yourself and work it for your own benefit. I don't suppose you'd also be interested in this sort of game, would you?"

I didn't want to say, "No" and risk losing out on the escape chapter. I couldn't imagine that the second situation could pose too much trouble. After all, it's not like these were life and death situations. "Sure, count me in, Jacob. I love adventure!"

Jacob seemed happy. He grinned, but it was sort of a mischievous smile. I picked up on his expression and asked, "What?"

"Nothing. I just think you're going to find these to be lots of fun. Both types of problem-solving are climactic chapters in the book. Jefferson thinks you'll do great. From what Josef told me about you, so do I."

With these words, I'd committed myself not only to what sounded like adventure leading to fame but, moreover, down the path of no return. IPM had me. I'd very soon become the pawn of competing players on a complicated three-tiered chessboard. How could I have ever thought I was so stinking smart at that age?

Maybe I was one of those unlucky guys who was born with no frontal lobe at all!

Axiom Thirty-Seven
Alibis distance prey intellectually from their pursuers.
Have a good alibi in case running doesn't work.

Jacob continued, "Josef said he noticed that you run around the campus a couple times a day. You must be in excellent shape. Can you also talk your way out of trouble if you need to?"

I stuck my chest out and paused for a moment, putting on a tone of arrogance. "Well, you see Jacob, I actually come from a long line of Martins, direct descendants of the Huns and the Vikings. Let me tell you about the time that my cousins set me up to get caught and then abandoned me when we were kids playing ding-dong-ditch-it! We were at this guy's house who they knew could probably outrun a wild horse."

I recounted the humorous story, and Jacob really seemed to be getting a good laugh about the guy chasing me across his yard and up the street. In fact, he almost appeared to be enjoying the tale of my peril and fear a little too much!

Then, I finished, "Yeah, I was eleven years old. My cousins had bets as to whether I'd pee my pants. But I showed them! I was the one who made the most out of that deal. I convinced the guy that I'd been at his doorstep calling on him to see if he needed someone to mow his lawn for the rest of the summer at $10 a pop. I ended up earning $70 over the next couple of months. Unlike my unfortunate conniving cousins, I was never out of ice-cream money. That hot sweaty summer I'd eat fudgsicles in front of them and taunt: 'Too bad for you guys that you set me up at Mr. Hogan's house!'"

I'd dramatically finish part of the gooey ice cream, while they gloated. Then, I'd inflict further emotional pain by throwing the half uneaten bar in the trash. I vindictively pushed my jealous audience into repeated spats of vulgarity.

They'd holler, "Hey! What the heck are you doing, Levi? If you don't want the rest of that, share it with us!"

I tasted the delight of my superiority among those who were older and who were thought to have been smarter. Oh, how sweet were those moments!

"Too bad you guys don't have a good paying job like mine!"

"The last time I chose to do that, however, they ganged up and beat the crap out of me."

Again, Jacob seemed oddly happy when he heard the part about me getting hurt. He was sure turning out to be a strange guy!

"I pulled myself up out of the dirt with the left-over part of an ice cream sandwich smeared all over my face. The memory of it all was worth every second of pain over the next few days. My black eye eventually went away, but my infamy has lived on for decades."

I thought I should enlighten him a little more about relational dynamics in the clan, "In our family, you had to think fast and be prepared to put a spin on things when you were in trouble. Everything seemed to boil down to trying to outsmart one another. If you messed with the wrong cousin at the wrong time, a butt-kicking awaited you. Because vengeance was a future certainty, you quickly developed those eyes in the back of your head that Mom told you about. We learned to wheel and deal, mastering the art of negotiation as a matter of self-preservation."

Jacob kept nodding politely. When I realized that I was going on endlessly, like Josef after playing chess, I concluded, "By the time we were all ten or so, each of us knew the difference between the taste of Dial and Ivory. If our parents thought we weren't being truthful, they lined us up with a bar of soap. This kind of punishment backfired, because it became the best training for us to invent better, more believable stories the next time around."

Jacob remarked, "That's quite a resume, Levi. I bet you're going to shine like a star in Jefferson's book. Hey, since you're so talented, why don't you come over sometime to play video games"

"Sure. That would be fun."

I began to realize something odd about Jacob during those few visits. He'd play for hours on end. It seemed as if the pastime consumed all of his waking hours when he wasn't working. A trash can in his apartment was overflowing with empty 2-liter Mtn. Dew bottles. This explained how he stayed awake all night, moving up to increasingly difficult levels in the game.

After several hours in his living room, I ascertained that my actual purpose in joining him wasn't for a meaningful social engagement, nor was it for the mutual enjoyment of his video game collection. Jacob became maniacally obsessed as he played. His demeanor probably worsened as he was amped up after guzzling copious amounts of highly caffeinated soda.

My first purpose in joining Jacob for the evening was to be beaten. I was intended as the fodder for his triumphs. To observe that he gloated after winning was an understatement.

Second of all, I served as his cheering section.

"Victory is bliss! Do you like how I did that, Levi? Watch me with the next one. You veer to the right like this and press the yellow button to survive. Look at how I got that guy! Wasn't that great?"

He really liked my enthusiasm, when I commented, "You're just amazing, Jacob!"

He glanced an excited smile back at me.

My third purpose in joining him was to manage his potty breaks. In the earliest generation of video games, it wasn't possible to pause the play feature. The programmers never figured that anyone could survive so long and still be on his first play.

Being the genius that he was, Jacob figured out a way to jam the controller with repeated movements and button depressions.

A desperate look came over his face as he thrust his controller into my hands. "Here, Levi. Hold this and press the red button continuously as you force the joystick toward the northeast sector of its movement."

I did as he said and asked, "Why?"

"I have to use the toilet, and those combined motions will stall the game."

"Okay."

He left the bathroom door open, and from the sounds of it, I expected a flood. When he returned, before commandeering control of the game, he downed another liter of soda.

"How will you ever sleep tonight, Jacob?"

"Sleep? Levi, it's Friday. School doesn't begin again until Monday."

"Never mind, Jacob. What was I thinking?"

I don't really know how many bottles he consumed that evening.

I'd been defeated by him and the game numerous times, but he was still on the first challenge using life token #1, with 3 more to spare. As the night progressed, I was honored to manage his controller several times when he relieved himself.

When I could play no more, he'd just gotten warmed up. The machine was hot and smelled like burning plastic. Jacob burned-out game consoles on a weekly basis. Then he'd hit every garage sale in town to scarf up replacements. The manufacturers hadn't anticipated one so addicted as Jacob.

As I said good night, he commented with delight on how poorly I'd done, but he suggested that with practice there was hope. Then, he asked me to bring him a bucket that was stashed behind the couch.

I saw a bit of liquid in the bottom, and caught a whiff. With disgust, I recognized the contents. I began to comment, "You're not going to use that, while you're playing to...?" But I didn't finish what I'd intended to ask. Jacob seemed to have his system of irrigation down pat. At that point, I made up my mind to buy him a catheter for Christmas. Being a practically minded fellow, he'd probably trim off the unnecessary length, tie it in a large knot, and use that part like one of those curly cue, sippy-straws.

Axiom Thirty-Eight
Someone is watching you.

It's funny how we're conditioned to dismiss certain kinds of thoughts. We read the axiom above and instantly rebound with defensive ideas like: "Nobody is watching me!" "Who would be watching me?" "Certainly, there is nobody watching me!" Axioms—valuable deposits of wisdom—might prove to be useful if we didn't so easily dismiss them. If we worked diligently to listen and find relevant applications, these valuable posits of wisdom might prove to be beneficial to our wellbeing. Why don't we instead naturally proceed through life being guided by the axiomatic questions: "Who is watching me now?" "What do they hope to find?" "How can I use the fact that someone has his/her eye on me in order to better my circumstances?"

The real point of the axiom isn't that we should drown ourselves in paranoia, but each of us needs to relearn what it means to be a learner. We miss many valuable lessons in life because we disregard the need for critical thought, and instead, we trust in our assumptions.

IPM helped me to understand that when I identify those individuals who are surveilling my life, I'm able to leverage their assumptions and inclinations. Rather than becoming exploited by others, I can plant ideas in their minds to serve my own purposes.

It should be obvious to thinking readers that someone is, of course, always watching us. The Almighty, parents, teachers, employers, peers, friends, and enemies, alike, observe us moment by moment and day by day. People with specific needs want to see how we might fit into their plans or may desire to ascertain how to defend themselves against us. From the point of figuring out what they're after, we might respond perceptively, having anticipated what they're looking for. While they observe, the opportunity exists to build a stage, craft a story, and to accomplish our own goals in their minds using their intellectual momentum to further shape their persuasions.

By the way, someone is watching you! Could it be the folks from IPM? What do they hope to find? What are you going to do with this knowledge?

Axiom Thirty-Nine
Test out your disguise in advance.

In the first escape challenge, I was sent down to New York City, about a two-hour bus ride from New Paltz. At precisely eleven a.m., I was instructed to be standing across the street from a certain embassy building in a chicken outfit. I remained silent and handed out bright yellow feathers to children and all who tried talking to me. No matter what happened, I was to remain out front, until three limousines showed up, and people began exiting the vehicles.

As a word of advice to those who may follow in my footsteps, be certain to try on the costume before you wear it for an hour and then attempt to run in it. I ended up with a bad, red rash, as they say, "where the sun doesn't shine."

Axiom Forty
Always beware of *fowl play.*

According to my watch, at about 11:38 a.m., just as had been explained, three limousines arrived. Those who looked to be important people got out. They were nicely dressed and their jewelry glittered in the morning sun. Little did I know that my actions were about to change the course of history in a third world nation. It would be more than a year before the actual purpose of these events would be revealed to me.

In the first twenty minutes, I'd drawn considerable attention. Several people watched me from the sidewalk, high-rise windows, and even with binoculars from the lower rooftops of adjacent buildings. Considering the looks of my costume, I hoped it wasn't turkey hunting season. I counted at least three embassy officials keeping track of my every move.

As the riders exited the limos, as instructed, I began doing jumping jacks, squawking, flapping my arms, and dancing around like an oversized crazed chicken. It was a commotion nobody could've missed or ignored. I ran back and forth screeching at the top of my lungs. I threw feathers into the air and pointed at the group of unsuspecting dignitaries standing between the limos and the embassy doors. Then I turned away and under the cover of my wing, I lit two strings of firecrackers. All were stunned and took cover between the cars, looking every which way and overhead. A crowd gathered quickly on both sides of the street and people poured out of the adjacent buildings.

After about forty-five seconds of seeming eternity, the riders retreated back into the limos, and the drivers burned rubber as they sped away. Understand that I thought what I'd been told to do was a prank. Although, somehow, I expected this to eventually involve a chase, I wasn't thinking that such apprehension would be awakened and enlivened in the would-be embassy visitors, or that they were going to flee. After all, I was just some nut dressed in a chicken outfit! It was a joke, or so, I thought.

What ensued, however, was nothing less than mayhem. There must have been a backstory to what had just occurred, but I had no idea what any of it was about. Dr. J was holding out on me. Instead of gawking at the knucklehead acting like an idiot in a bird costume, men from the embassy shouted, "Get that guy!"

Axiom Forty-One
"Run Forrest Run!"
~ Forrest Gump ~

Three, angry looking, well-dressed men rushed toward me, dodging cars and pedestrian traffic.

"You there! Stop!"

They were swearing up a storm as they plowed forward, and I could see that something serious was happening!

From that point, I did just as I was instructed. I ran. A surge of adrenaline hit me like a rocket. I ran like I never ran before, leaving a trail of discarded pieces of chicken outfit flittering in the wind, littering the sidewalk behind me.

They yelled, "Running is useless! Get back here!"

I knew that the three suits clad with leather soles were no match for my Brooks running shoes.

As I rounded the first corner, my heart was beating hard. I didn't see the spike-topped, three-foot-high, metal fence and plowed straight into it. I couldn't move. I whipped off the mask and realized that my outfit was impaled on the railing. I pushed back with all my strength tearing the costume from top to bottom, exposing my body from chest to thigh. One of the suits got close enough to grab a handful of feathers from my back.

I lurched forward and booked down the stairs into the subway. Hurdling over the turnstile, I bolted through the tunnel straight into the open doors of the first car in view. I took a left and ran into the next train carriage, as I saw the three stooges, who gave chase, jumping on the same train several cabins down the line. When we began moving, I clenched my fingers between the doors and forced them open far enough to vault back onto the platform and scurry over to the next train. Its doors shut immediately, trapping the feathery tail of my costume. I was heaving for breath, checking over my shoulder, thinking about the crazy scene I'd created. Nevertheless, all that mattered was that my pursuers were now on a different line, heading in the opposite direction. I worked hard to catch my breath. It had been a close call. I sure hoped Dr. J wasn't looking for the return of his outlandish attire!

As I proceeded into Brooklyn, I removed the rest of my disguise and put on new clothing from the duffle bag. It's funny how nobody seems to watch or care about a person who strips down to his underwear and changes clothes on the N.Y. City subway! I abandoned the bag, got out at the next stop, ran up the stairs, hailed a cab, rode to Manhattan, got back on the train, and proceeded to repeat this sort of activity for several hours.

I didn't know anything about how Dr. J had set that chase up, but one thing I knew for sure was that I didn't want to see those embassy guys ever again!

I'd started the day with a big wad of cash to use for cabs, bus fares, and subway tokens. I was hoping to be able to keep some of it when I began, but I'd paid for so many rides back and forth across New York, Manhattan, and Brooklyn that it was nearly gone when I arrived at the Trailways Bus Station. Lamenting that the outfit was gone before getting a photo for the book, I was, however, relieved to catch my ride back up to New Paltz.

Axiom Forty-Two
Always control the engagement.

There are different ways to manage our interactions with others. Sometimes you want people to think you're managing the engagement and other times you don't. The appearance of either strength or weakness can provide the effective means to control others. We were taught at IPM that no matter what, it was imperative that we always maintained power over the situations in which we found ourselves.

This was the premise that afforded us important advantages to set people up. A target's deepest convictions about what he thought his circumstances looked like became our springboards into action.

IPMers learned to affect people's awareness in different ways. Depending upon the propensities of the subject, control might also be managed by the selective appearance of sadness, confusion, fear, doubt, etc. The goal was making other people's likely behavior and choices predictable.

Patient observation and gathering of facts about an individual gave way to greater effectiveness in altering the course of his life. We learned to increasingly examine and test our targets to better assure our desired outcomes.

The dynamic of change was enhanced through the use of props, as was the case with the parties hosted by Dr. Jefferson. We used artifacts such as family photos, framed credentials, stories, others' incidental discoveries, and a plethora of strategies leading our victims to make false, inferential conclusions. Once they became convinced that a certain positively or negatively charged situation existed, we knew what action they were likely to take when we exposed them to a set of stimuli. Therefore, specific kinds of tools were judiciously placed within range of their senses to subtly convince them of whatever we needed them to believe. Eventually, in the best setups, the target's own discoveries, no matter how false all of them were, became the fulcrum for IPM's actions.

Whatever the backstory might have been, those guys from the embassy had been well primed and were ripe were for the picking. The timing and appearance of the chicken had a specific meaning in their minds, provoking fear, anger, and the frantic compulsion to escape. Just as it had been predicted, they reacted and fled. This proved they were concerned about something very serious. In the ensuing chase, there could be no doubt that my pursuers were out for blood.

Moving a target through the stages between exposure to erroneous information and onward toward motivated action was a careful process that couldn't be rushed. Falsehood couldn't be force-fed. The target had to be courted through exposure to evidence, allowed to swallow and digest erroneous information, and then process all of this at his own pace. Like the growing layers of an onion, formative values and basic needs were overlaid with assumptions based on inferences. Convincing testimonies and visual pieces of evidence further led the prey toward what they thought were their own conclusions.

The procedure of setting a person up was like winding up a rubber band. When it was fully wound, dynamic tension was instilled in the object. Then, the right provocation could cause it to snap and unleash its torrent of stored energy; only for our targets to find themselves landing in even worse predicaments. In the end, they exhausted themselves emotionally. Depleted of energy, resources, and lacking the wherewithal to keep fighting, they were consumed by their worst fears. Once started, the dominoes continued tumbling in a prescribed path, eventually, leading each target to self-destruction.

Age played a factor in all of this. Older subjects required slow deliberate care. Immaturity and character flaws helped speed the processes. We used a wide degree of different emotional pressures, combined with good or bad discoveries to precipitate concern that would eventually move them to action.

For example, a guy would find out his wife was having an affair. In the plan to catch her in the act, he'd make an even worse discovery and become convinced that his business partners were embezzling. After further investigation, he'd discover some outside, adversarial force threatening to destroy him. Scenarios went from bad, to worse, to unfathomable, until the criminal target resorted to drastic measures that also exposed him for who and what he was. At some point along the way, he'd meet an IPM executive, posing as someone with opportunities and solutions to remedy his problems.

That's when the real fun began. We were there just in time to seal his doom. Mind you, however terrible this sounds, the players we took out were the wickedest among humankind.

High school boys with poorly developed frontal lobes were perhaps the easiest and quickest people to set up. We complimented them on how smart or talented they supposedly were. Immediately, in many cases, we had instant, trusting friends. Then, we suggested doing some crazy things, asserting that these activities would be adventurous, challenging, and fun. Very quickly our prey became pawns for our bidding. Before long, they were eating out of our hands. Feeling confident in their abilities, they'd naively take on challenges, like causing a commotion in a chicken outfit. Some of them managed to get a clue, only while they were running for their lives!

Axiom Forty-Three
Watch for those who will play your ego.

"Stan the Man" was a cool guy in a neighboring high school called "Sojourner Truth," located ten miles from Bodega High. I met him through our mutual friend Mike Spires. Even though I was a nerd in my own town, Stan thought I was cool. It felt good for a change to have someone think highly of me.

Stan and some guys took me down to the Coltonville trestle bridge that spanned the Fargus River.

He told everyone, "Martin can do it!" He looked at me. "Levi, you're a good swimmer, aren't you?"

Whether I really was or not, I nodded, "Yeah, man. Why?"

"Because you gotta' jump. I know you can do it!"

I nervously climbed to the top of the rusted metal frame, high above the roadway and looked down at the water. My first thought was "OH, CRAP!" It was so stinking high above the river! I knew I better do it fast without thinking about it much longer, or I'd never jump.

I shouted, "Okay, here goes!" I sailed forward and for a split second, I heard this massive "SWOOSH" as the air rushed past my ears. Then, I felt the freezing cold water flood over and surround me. I'd held my breath, and as I spread my arms and legs, I came to a stop and pushed back toward the daylight. I couldn't wait to resurface into the fresh air. It turned out to be a blast.

Had Stan not been working my ego, I probably would never have experienced the flight and launched my body from high atop the trestle. It was a clever way of manipulating a guy like me, who sometimes lived for the admiration and approval of others. I knew that Stan thought I was cool, and I didn't want to lose my position of esteem in his mind.

This is a common reason why popular kids and adults become the pawns of others. Inwardly, the value of maintaining social status is more highly placed than their own sense of self-preservation. Assuredly, in my case, the questionable decision was due to my underdeveloped frontal lobe. In my brain, the desire for fame trumped common sense. In the absence of my ability to think critically, calling bright ideas into question, the desire for recognition became the dictator of my decision, enticing me to take foolish risks.

Later, I thought about that event, and I was glad that I lived much of my life as a nerd in my own high school. I maintained the freedom to be free as a leader, because I didn't have a high-minded reputation to lose.

Having accepted their individual, cultural, and social independence, nerds are empowered decisively to rise above the morass of dramatic entanglements that surround them.

If there was a second important lesson in all of this, I learned that jumping off bridges was wicked fun! Smaller bridges led to higher ones. Water landings eventuated in bungee jumping; the higher the better. And these experiences were foundational to leaping from airplanes. Mom would've clipped my wings, but thankfully, she never knew.

Axiom Forty-Four
Whether you're going with or against the flow, your goal is to control the flow.

I'd found tremendous satisfaction with the challenges for Jefferson's book. I was spurred on by the enticement that I'd soon be a star player in the narrative. It felt good to be alive.

Gradually, however, as I moved from one challenge to the next, I began feeling like a cork bobbing aimlessly down a river. Although there had never been so much excitement in my life, and the contests were way more fun than doing homework, I had an unusual realization one morning. I apprehended the conclusion that I was no longer the person in control of my life.

Dr. J, or an M.C., might show up at any moment, and I was always running here and there for them (literally). Being important to somebody else made me feel good. But still, the sense of being someone else's puppet gave way to deeper questions. "What were all these pranks really about? How would they be transformed into a literary form? Was Oprah going to invite me on her show?"

When it all began, I thought I was working my way into a fraternity. I'd followed the steppingstones and had bounded over the hurdles toward what I'd thought was a position of respect in a collegiate hierarchy of brothers. Then, I discovered that these antics were the supporting research for a book. In each set of understandings, I wanted to become a more significant part of Josef and Jacob's world. They were very cool guys, although, I was beginning to catch on to the fact that Jacob had some issues. He tended to treat me strangely.

I never would have guessed where any of this was actually leading. Mom and Dad had always been aware of my fascination with fire, but what would they have thought about my eventual identity as a full-fledged arsonist? In less than 100 days I'd prove myself as such and worse. Could they have pictured me as a vigilante? What would Dad say about my foreign imprisonment by a warlord involved in human trafficking? No threat of discipline they'd ever thought of could've saved me from the destiny of my footsteps over the next several months!

Axiom Forty-Five
Think twice. Don't jump to conclusions.

This was a formative lesson in mind games. In my early experiences with Dr. Jefferson, his peers, and the IPM Corporation, there were many tricky challenges. Some might even sound impossible. Often, there were clues to figure out in order to discover the proper solution. As time went on, they introduced increasing levels of difficulty. One's interpretation of semantics affected the expected course of action.

On a cold winter day, you might be instructed, "Stick out your tongue and touch the flagpole." The losers were ones who ended up glued to the frozen metal rod. The winners reached over and made contact with a dry hand or finger, while sticking their tongue out at the M.C.

Axiom Forty-Six
Nothing is impossible!
Dismiss and banish the concept of impossibility.

I stood gathered with three other students and M.C., Jacob outside the Old Main Building. We were on the far side of the campus away from my dorm. It was me, two new guys and the $5 chick from the first party. I did a doubletake at her again because she looked familiar.

Jacob began, "Today's challenge is one of getting back to each of your dormitories without your feet ever touching the ground."

We looked at each other and smiled, because the challenge sounded ridiculous. One of the other two guys was picking up one boot off the ground then the other and looking comically at his feet as he did so. He remarked to his friend and the rest of us, "Jacob, that's crazy!"

The other student shook his head in agreement.

"Yeah, nobody can do that! It's impossible."

The first asked, "Have you been drinking, Jacob? This is insane!"

I could tell that the M.C. didn't take kindly to being made fun of. He replied, "Okay. Thank you, gentlemen. Then, that's all for you today."

The pair looked at one another, shrugged, and then they wandered off laughing and making small talk about how stupid the whole idea was.

Jacob lamented, "Sadly, those guys are philosophical prisoners in the rationalistic, Aristotelian perspective called 'impossibility.' Nothing is impossible."

Unbeknownst to Jacob's detractors, then and there, both had forfeited their potential futures with one of the most astounding organizations on the planet. Perhaps the only impossibility was for those whose minds were framed in the construct of impossibility to coexist with others who continually defied impossibility.

Early, thoughtless, surrender unveiled potentials' incompatibility with the theoretical underpinnings of IPM. Low-level challenges like this one were followed by designs requiring even more complex thinking strategies.

Later, in instances when I played the "Dr. Jefferson" role in collegiate recruiting, I learned that in many cases every potential recruit was eliminated before the end of the semester. The first time this happened, I was really bummed about all our wasted efforts.

Jack consoled me, "Recruiting isn't about finding talented students skilled enough to join our ranks, it's about identifying those individuals whom IPM can't do without."

It was necessary for the company to staff its business selectively with a very particular kind of participant. In retrospect, we were kind of a circus collection. Eventually, you'll be introduced to all the players. Each of us had special talents that made us indispensable.

Those who would eventually triumph in IPM's tests were optimists. They were creative, critical thinkers, guided by the premise, "All things are possible." This intellectual foundation was the launch pad for achievement.

Whoever it was that first became convinced of the vicious lie of "impossibility" was the victim of hopelessness, helplessness, and fear. False, restrictive notions like these perpetuated generations of sadness and disappointment in the world.

Fundamental intellectual structures that gave way to phrases, like, "I can't do that," had to be eradicated from our minds. They were necessarily replaced with the reflective, investigative attitudes and motivated statements such as, "Let's get to work on the problem. We can figure this out!"

I recall that as a lazy, snotty nosed, seven-year-old I was defiantly mouthing off to my mother, "I don't know how to make the bed!" I was such an imbecile! I regret that she or anyone ever had to put up with me. Her method of motivation was simple. She spoke the perilous words, "Get the belt!"

Crap! I'd heard the command many times as a kid. The result was never a pretty sight. Once again, my evil attitude had failed to help me get my way avoiding work.

Mom doubled the leather strap over and held it ready in her right hand as she lightly tapped it on her left. She stared me down and nodded at the bed. Right then and there, I got to work straightening those sheets and blankets! If my brain didn't know what was good for me, my butt sure did!

One could find the way to do anything with the proper motivation, consideration, research, resources, attitude, and application of technology. My parents' brave discipline made me who I am. Thank the Almighty! Can I hear an "Amen!"?

Axiom Forty-Seven

Angry people are easy to make angrier.

On that note, before I go on to explain just how I resolved the not-so-impossible problem of getting back to my dorm without my feet touching the ground, I should mention a relevant story about my friend "Old Brass." His connections with military intel provided the prodding that eventually led to the writing of this book. He once paid me a high compliment, even though he didn't mean it to be taken that way.

First, let me say that he lived next door. There was a spot in the yard near our property lines where he'd worn out the grass from constantly poking his nose in my business.

Well, Old Brass always saw me doing things at our home like rewiring, changing structural beams and altering the layout of the house. He frequently overheard me advising mutual acquaintances on corporate downsizing, investment, mortgage, and leasing strategies.

I once explained to a friend how to start a nutritional product line, emphasizing the value of building a strong brand name, and then accompanied this with a well-developed marketing plan.

"You see, having a valuable product to sell is only a small part of the business component."

Old Brass cut in, "Levi, you think you know everything! Don't you?"

I replied, "Think about it. Competitors can steal your recipes or improve upon them, but eventually what you hope to sell is the trademarked brand."

Our mutual friend replied, "I see now. The bigger money isn't in the individual products, it's in the conglomerate machine you build."

My neighbor was flabbergasted, "Where in the world did you learn to think of all this stuff? Was it from studying a computer mogul like Marcus Ray Monroe?"

Have you ever had a dentist hit a nerve that sent you flying up, out of the chair? That's exactly what Old Brass' comment about Monroe had done! The story is probably a thousand pages ahead if I ever manage to make it that far. Was what he said a mere coincidence or a careless slip of the tongue?

I looked at him squarely and decided on the latter. Brass had just revealed something. I now had good reason and perhaps evidence to suspect there was more to his seemingly random appearance and his existence in my life as a next door neighbor.

As if he'd realized his error just a moment too late, he tried to cover for it, but it didn't come of so well.

He stammered, "One day, the kinds of things you say are going to be like Evangel DeMichael's bragging that he was the best hitter in the league; only to be struck out almost continually for a season."

The comment about the baseball player was unnecessary and really didn't contribute to his point. It was obvious that Brass was trying to recover, but it was too late. He fumbled, and now, I knew my life probably depended on keeping a close eye on him. Only someone who'd been watching and knew the histories of my alter identities and aliases might have made a connection between me and Monroe! These many years after I thought my past was buried, had it now come back to haunt me?

I'd played so many different kinds of roles while working projects for IPM that I knew a little bit about most everything. In order to fake being a consultant in quite a number of different industries, I had to study their best practices, histories of development, product testing, distribution channels, and marketing. Those five areas of concern were the central foci as I prepared to take on aliases in IPM's projects.

At one point I was involved in three simultaneous jobs, posing as a chemical consultant in the dish soap industry, a venture capitalist from a prominent banking organization, and even as a small-time gangster in Chicago. You better believe that even criminals have "best practices." If you knew the ropes, you might not get shot! Spies who survive in the trade, become excellent researchers.

For all my life, I'd been an avid reader and a lifetime learner. I freely offered what I'd acquired as an advantage to others.

Despite who he might or might not be, why these things pissed off Brass so much, I'll never know! The more he listened in on my schemes the more scornful and critical he became. I'd heard that a malady in older men is shrinkage of the brain. The more shriveled it becomes, the more bad-tempered they tend to act.

Because of this, my neighbor was easy to mess with. I admit that occasionally, I enjoyed pushing his buttons. Still, I did try to be a good friend whenever possible. One time he followed my advice on a profitable way to end an automotive lease. He earned $3,000, instead of paying the $2,000 for his mileage overage. He did treat me kindly for that advice.

Because of that $5k, however, and since he was just a cantankerous old coot who should've kept his nose on his own side of the fence, every now and again I took liberty in harassing him. I encouraged my neighbor that it kept him young. I think he enjoyed the negative attention from time to time. He and I lived in a playful state of mutual animosity. Now and again, we shared a few laughs. I used to cajole him, "You know, I love you?" He'd smile and give me that troublemaker kind of grin. I'd say, "Tell your wife that Levi says, 'Thanks for putting up with you!'" He always said, "I will!" Did Old Brass really understand the implications of that last request?

Anyway, one day my neighbor announced in a sarcastic tone, "Levi, you remind me of 'Dr. Emmet Brown' from the movie *Back to the Future* and his 'Flux Capacitor.' You're just like Brown! You're not afraid of anything!" He echoed the voice of Durlong, whom I'd heard say something similar, years earlier. Eventually, we'll get to all that. For now, though, to understand the relevance of the mention of my neighbor, Old Brass closed the discussion asking, "Don't you ever think anything is impossible?"

Axiom Forty-Eight
Give yourself time to think.
If you haven't had time to reflect,
don't feel compelled to speak.

Impulsivity was a greatly loathed character flaw among IPMers. It was the fatal weakness that led to the downfall of the majority of IPM's targets. It was more respectable for an IPMer to be taken down while attempting to formulate a successful plan, rather than making oneself the victim of his own shortsighted haste.

Back on the steps of Old Main, due to the surrender and forfeiture of our two shortsighted peers, it was up to the $5 deal chick and me to figure out a workable solution to Jacob's challenge. She and I stood there cogitating. I really wanted to be first to get whatever brownie points were available, and it turned out to be my lucky day.

I approached Jacob and with a hushed voice and explained, "I think I can do this on my bike."

He asked, "What about stairs or going through a building? Won't you wreck your bike or your face?"

I stuck my chest out, "Well now, Jacob, you're talking to Levi Martin! Stairways go downhill and buildings have elevators. You decide the path, and I'll make it from Old Main back to my dorm room."

Since each of our theoretical solutions were ultimately aimed at the design of individual tests, the girl and I didn't share our ideas. I didn't learn that her remedy had been to have the football team carry her back until one of the following semesters.

At 9 o'clock the next morning, Jacob gave me a map of the expected route. Amidst the hustle and bustle of students, I got on my candy-apple red Schwinn 10-speed and was psyched for the challenge. I flew away from Old Main on the trail prescribed by the M.C., taking me down two fairly steep exterior stairways that connected the front of the art building to the side entrance of the second level of the Student Union Building (SUB).

As a kid, I'd learned it was survivable to traverse a flight of steps on a bike. My cousin attempted to terrorize me, while I sat on his bike rack holding on for dear life.

I rode right up to the doorway of the SUB, bumped the door jamb, balanced carefully, reached and pulled the door open, made my way into the building, rode around the hallway past the bookstore to the elevator, went to the ground level, while leaning on the wall inside the elevator, traversed the hall and bumped the crash hardware on the exit door, went out into the street tunnel and took a left. People looked at me a little bit funny, but then again, we were all college students, and we were all in a hurry.

I headed over the second footbridge connecting student housing with the cafeteria and eventually coasted into the laundry area in the back, lower level of LeFevre Hall. Then, I took the elevator upstairs and made it all the way into our suite.

I'd tell you the exact time that it took, but that's become classified information.

"Okay, Levi, your time was good, and you made it according to the rules."

He was looking at me a little oddly, and I smiled back, asking, "What is it, Jacob?"

He said, "To be honest, it surprised me when you made it safely down the stairs to the SUB."

I bragged, "Well, ya' knew all along ya' were dealin' with *Levi Martin; doggone it all anyway!* What did ya' expect?" I began to laugh, but strangely, he didn't share appreciation over my humorous response.

So, I got all serious looking and asked, "Were you hoping I'd have a wreck and break my neck?"

M.C. Jacob didn't answer immediately, but finally commented, "You did well in the low-level challenge. We'll see how you progress."

Rubbing my hands together, I said, "Well, bring em' on!"

"Before we start the next test, you have to repeat the same bike route, and cut your time in half."

I knew I'd better not object, saying something stupid like, "That's impossible!" Instead, I repeated his statement with incredulity, "Cut my time in half?"

He replied tersely, "That's right, Levi! Can you do that?"

"Well, if I'd known you were going to ask me that ahead of time, I'd have relaxed on my first jaunt." Then, I added, "Maybe you're just trying to get me killed on those last two steep sets of stairs."

This time he replied to my question, offering an evil grin and saying, "You're very perceptive, Levi."

Axiom Forty-Nine
Keep your body in good shape.

Unlike Wendell, I wasn't very athletic before coming to college. Realizing that the escapes were physically demanding, I thought I could kill two birds with one stone and get credits for taking a jogging class. Even so, I couldn't really seem to be able to jog. Instead, as it turned out, I actually took up running. At my peak, I ran three miles around the campus early in the morning and again in the afternoon.

In retrospect, it's interesting how so many people on the campus recognized me because of my daily routine. I'd meet someone at a party and they'd say, "Hey, aren't you the guy who runs?" After so many trips from Old Main to my dorm on the Schwinn, I was rather disappointed that they hadn't remembered me for riding my bike down the campus stairs.

I worked hard and practiced that same course repeatedly at all hours of the night and day. I managed, quite frequently, to startle and frighten pedestrians. Nevertheless, I'd made the first run in such a short amount of time, it was difficult to improve my pace.

Then, one day I reconsidered the M.C.'s challenge. I'd rashly interpreted the overt semantics of his comment as having to do solely with speed. There was another way to accomplish his challenge.

Jacob stopped by my dorm to see if I'd help with an upcoming party one evening and I took out a sheet of paper with the printed phrase "MY TIME." I said, "Okay, Jacob, watch this!" As he looked at me, I used scissors and cut "MY TIME" in half. The M.C. smiled and said, "Touché! Where there's a will, there's a Levi!"

Axiom Fifty
Running is something, but endurance is everything.

"How many miles can you run steadily? How fast can you do that?"

These were the questions posed by Dr. Jefferson on a sunny spring morning over a ham and cheese omelet. He'd taken me out for breakfast at the local diner. I can guess accurately that he already knew my routine of three miles twice a day. I wasn't super-fast and averaged only an eight-minute mile. I could keep up with a seven-minute runner, and with adrenaline, I could manage six minutes and some change.

But, since, I didn't want to press my limits, I kept my estimate easily within what I knew I could produce. "I can do about three miles in twenty-four minutes."

Dr. J further inquired, "Would you like to make a hundred dollars?" Of course, anyone could have predicted the answer to the question, if they knew they were dealing with an authentic college student!

Axiom Fifty-One
Innocence is bliss.
Maintain your innocence.

At this time, I didn't realize that my actions would be just a small part of a larger operation that had been in various states of planning for the past several months. Since I was completely unaware of IPM and its objectives, I repeatedly viewed Jefferson's challenges as pranks he was playing on friends or associates. This time his benevolence included covering my expenses as part of the deal.

Had I been caught, in what one week later became the ground race for my life, I wouldn't have been able to tell my captors anything of value, because "Dr. Elias Jefferson" didn't actually exist. I was soon to discover that I knew him only by this alias.

Axiom Fifty-Two
Do your homework.

I received some traveling cash and went to an old municipal airport in Upstate N.Y. It had no security, and this was decades before the events of 9/11. Like most facilities of its kind, it was surrounded by expansive fields.

I was given a fat envelope jammed with Monopoly money, and the instructions were simple. Hike through the field to the hangar. Find "Joe." Give him the envelope, and then run back toward the town where a ride back to New Paltz would be waiting. It all sounded easy enough.

Upon further inquiry, I learned that Joe was in his mid-40s and not in the best shape. I didn't want to get caught by an Olympic runner, so I was doing my homework. Perhaps if I'd really been smart, I'd have asked a few more questions, like, "What in the world am I doing this for?" and "Does Joe happen to be a psychotic nut?" That's exactly what he turned out to be! Obviously, my frontal lobe was still developing.

~ An Aside from Elizabeth Angela Martin ~

Mom had done her best to help Wendell and I steer clear from any kind of nonsense that might have cost us life or limb, but some lessons are only learned through the experience of pain or loss. There we were squared off with Mom holding the belt and it didn't look good for our rear ends.

Wendell and I had taken shopping carts from Bellmont's and were racing down the long steep hill toward Main Street. The front wheels began to wobble, we collided, and my cart spun toward the curb and tore into the side of a car scraping it up really good. Wendell hit the fender of the one in front and our fun was over as fast as it had begun.

Oh, did I mention they were both police cars?

She began, "How - many - times - have - I - warned - you - boys?"

Man alive, did we ever know we were in big trouble when Mom left that little pause between each word.

"Just - wait - until - your - father - gets - home!"

DANG! It was going to be another night of double jeopardy! My little brother and I seemed to get ourselves into a mess like this two or three times per year; not very pretty.

She hollered, "Haven't your father and I raised you with common sense?" She pointed at us, "Don't tell me you don't know better! You've got to think ahead because one of these days you're going to get yourselves killed!"

What is it about common sense that no matter how many times Mom and Dad tried to tell us, we could only learn from experience?

Axiom Fifty-Three
Mind the details of your original plan.

There I was at sunrise, almost to the building, crawling through the weeds. At that moment, I was ahead of schedule, which I felt was a good thing. I thought I was so stinking cool, sneaking around to make $100! I went under the barbed wire cow fence, stood up and walked across the pavement to the hangar. I was figuring I'd just walk inside and ask for Joe, however, when I rounded the corner, I unexpectedly came face to face with the man. We were about the same height, but he had some meat on his bones. I was skinny as a rail. We scared the crap out of each other.

Joe lurched back shouting, "Holy Cow! Who the #$@%& are you?"

I almost fell over! For my own part, I was trying to suck my heavily pounding heart down out of my throat and back into my chest. I could hardly breathe. I had no words to speak, just gasps of air, as I tried to regain my composure.

I think I managed, "Argh hup!" and trailed off with a wheeze-like, squealing sound.

He could tell that I was as surprised as him to meet another living soul out there this early in the morning.

I finally muttered the faint inquiry, "Joe?"

I'd lost all control of the engagement and struggled to regain my sense of the mission. This wasn't happening the way I'd expected. I was planning on calmly finding Joe sitting in his office behind a desk. But, I was early, and that changed everything.

Being unable to say much more due to my startled condition, I just held up the envelope and shoved it toward him.

He asked, "For me?" and I shook my head affirmatively.

He looked perplexed.

"Is it a payment?"

I kept nodding as he took it from my hands.

Finally, I mumbled, "Yeah, well, kind of."

Then, sensing danger, I turned and ran like the wind. I don't remember how I even navigated the barbed wire fence. Did I jump over it or climb through it? Only the angels know for certain! I raced so hard and fast that I recall not even feeling my legs and feet beneath me. I was like a bird in flight.

Axiom Fifty-Four
Take seriously the face value
of the instructions you receive.

Here's the odd thing about learning from experience. Even though the whole challenge with Dr. J had begun with the query about my ability to run, I'd never really expected that Joe was going to chase me; not for what seemed to me at the time to be a mindless prank.

Joe was in better shape than I'd anticipated. I could hear the thud of his feet in the long grass behind me. He shouted, screamed, yelled, and threatened, "Your ass is grass! I'm gonna' rip your &%#@$ head off!"

I found the slightest bit of humor in his adamant command, "Get the hell back here! Now!"

What in the world was he thinking?

Had I not been in a race for my life, I might have hollered back, "Sure! Stop and wait right there. I'll be back in a quick five!"

I'd cleared the field and crossed the road, knowing that I only had a block and a half to go before I'd find safety in the waiting ride. Hopefully the driver was ready to put the pedal to the metal.

Meanwhile, I was astonished that Joe remained hot on my tail. Although I'd gained ground, extending the substantial distance between us, I still heard his vulgar threats detailing several forms of bodily injury he intended to inflict upon me.

I rounded the corner of the large, red building, the landmark for my rendezvous, but to my exceeding disappointment there was no car. Immediately, I was stunned in disbelief! NO CAR? NO WAY!

Somehow, Joe appeared to have grown to twice his size and now seemed even angrier. He was used to getting his way. He was still moving toward me with remarkable speed and both nostrils flaring. The gap between us closed slightly, as I moved in a wide circular pattern to see if I had missed my ride through a logistical error. It was then that the thought occurred to me, "Maybe Dr. J should've also included Park Place, Boardwalk, and some hotels with all the play money in that envelope!"

I was breathing hard and chanced a glance at my watch. I was in the right place at the wrong time. The driver wasn't scheduled to arrive for another ten minutes.

Axiom Fifty-Five
Remember that people are not always predictable.

I hadn't expected Joe's endurance. So, I kept on running straight up the street. I had no idea what the whole envelope thing was all about, but suddenly, the hundred-dollar part of the challenge seemed insignificant.

This was about to become like the dream where you're being chased by the big, ugly monster, but your feet only worked in slow motion. Rather than staying in plain view, where I might be found by my driver, I decided it was a safer bet to extend my life if I were to weave through a few yards so that I might lose Joe.

One day I'm going to go back and examine just how far I ran using Google Earth. It was a long, long way, much more than three miles. Near the end of it, Joe finally pooped out. I did too, but I was far enough out of his reach.

I was catching my breath when I heard tires squealing, and I felt relief knowing my ride had found me. But no! No way! It was Psycho-Joe in a Dodge Charger barreling through the neighborhood, and I was the deer in his headlights.

I felt like the extra in the weekly show who wasn't going to be part of the next episode. It's when I remembered lots of things at once. Speed isn't everything, agility can count for more. I pictured myself as a very skinny bullfighter about to take on a raging, green Encino. Joe's car, or whoever it belonged to, couldn't navigate physical barriers like I could; well, so I thought. In a trial by fire chase, Joe proved I was wrong and took down a whole string of laundry and fences in the process. Had this guy's mind been tortured by an infinite number of game losses as a child?

Someone should warn the manufacturer to put a disclaimer on the box!

I hurdled over three different chain-link fences, zigzagging through a myriad of flowerbeds, gardens, and lawns. Each turn cost Joe both speed and momentum. It was moments after attempting to plow through the third chain link fence that the raging bull became stuck. Boy did he ever tear up that guy's yard! I was another block away when I heard sirens heading back in Joe's direction.

Did I mention anything about prayer? Man, was I ever praying! My heart was beating so hard that my head was throbbing. I was exhausted. I doubled back around to the red building and walked to the car that had arrived sometime during the cat and mouse mayhem. I got in the back seat casually and laid down.

"Everything go okay?" the driver asked nonchalantly.

"Yep," was all I said the whole way back to college.

As I laid across the back seat for the ride home, something hit me that gave me an eerie feeling. Joe had a ghostly and unmistakable resemblance to the M.C. Josef. Josef was considerably thinner, but they could've been brothers or almost twins. The whole event had knocked me for a loop. I was emotionally and physically spent.

As I got out of the door, the driver reached back and handed me a crisp $100 bill. I think that experience caused my frontal lobe to begin growing a little faster.

Axiom Fifty-Six
When you're young, listen to your gut.
In your middle years, trust your gut.
When you get older, suck in your gut.

I began to really wonder about the point of these crazy excursions. Once again, I'd nearly gotten my face pulverized by an issue-laden stranger. Would I have lived to meet Oprah in the book deal if Joe had caught me? The deranged man definitely meant business!

I began to wonder more about Dr. J. He seldom asked for details pertaining to his research and writing. After a few chases, in keeping with Jacob's prediction, the escapes became increasingly challenging and my pursuers were equally out for blood. The denial that clouded my mind was fading. Was there some alternate reason that Jefferson was so interested in me? He was obviously using me to do some dirty work. Why?

The number of questions in my mind were mounting. Who did Jefferson work for? Why had Josef so suddenly disappeared? Whatever happened to my I.Q. test? A sense of ambiguity hung like a fog in my mind. I had a strange feeling about the ongoing challenges and wondered where all this might lead.

Axiom Fifty-Seven
Even when you're not smart, pretend.
There's always hope.

My geology professor, Dr. Adler, wasn't particularly fond of me. Perhaps if I'd done my homework more often and had something valuable to contribute in the classroom, his attitude would have been different. Flying by the seat of my pants, I did my best to pass his course, but I was nobody's perfect student in those days. That's a polite way of admitting that I was nearly a complete failure. A time of academic growth and change would eventually become part of my destiny, but that eventuality lay beyond the horizon of my experiences at New Paltz.

I later discovered that most of those involved with IPM had master's degrees. Education was highly valued. I was fortunate that they weren't looking for straight "A" students at the start. I most definitely didn't prove myself to be a brainiac during my bachelor's degree, barely graduating with the strong "C+" 2.75 cumulative average. The only respectable grades I received were in the basket weaving courses. I was pathetic. I tried, but I didn't have a clue how to study or know how to excel in the education system back in those days. Sometimes, I worked hard but never smart. Aptitude lay somewhere over the horizon with growth in my own maturity. Despite this reality and mostly because of Dr. Jefferson's intervention, I was about to be moved very near to the head of the class.

Axiom Fifty-Eight
When surprised, don't be taken captive.

So, one day we were working in a geology lab. It was a paleontology course, and the students were all busy beside me looking at trays full of fossils. We were trying to learn their characteristics and attempting to categorize each of them by kingdom, phylum, class, order, genus, and species; down to the lowest identifiable detail.

Dr. Adler strolled in looking all official and speaking in a different tone of voice than we were used to hearing. There following him was Dr. Jefferson, wearing a stylish suit and carrying a leather attaché case with a white envelope in his hand.

I was glad to see Dr. J again. By the way they conversed and smiled as they entered, I thought they must have been friends. Jefferson gave me a quick nod, squinted his eyes and slowly shook his head. I could tell that he didn't want me to recognize him in front of the professor. I stayed about my work and was surprised when I was suddenly being introduced to Dr. Jefferson; but now by a new name.

"Levi, I'd like you to meet 'Pete Sommers,' from the Shilling Oil Corporation. He's come to discuss your correspondences with them. They like your ideas and want to consider you for a work-study program."

I almost blew it by asking, "Are you kidding?" Luckily, I swallowed my words and narrowly maintained my composure. I played along.

Axiom Fifty-Nine
Paradoxes may be purposeful.
Listen carefully and respond in-kind.

Dr. Jefferson, who was now "Pete Sommers" spoke next. He said the strangest thing. "Your professor and I go way back. We went to different high schools together." Dr. Adler gave Pete a quizzical, odd look while tilting his head to the side. I smiled trying to figure all of this out. I was becoming increasingly confused and the event was turning surreal.

There was a pause for a moment, and then Dr. Jefferson or Pete Sommers or whoever he was looked at my professor and said, "Oh, I'm just joking around."

This was my first exposure to an IPM paradox, the proverbial secret handshake commonly used in the field to identify other operatives. IPM had many ongoing initiatives and was substantial in size when counting the subsidiary front organizations. Dr. J tested and confirmed his suspicion, by the perplexed look on Dr. Adler's face. He knew it was safe to proceed with his ruse. However, had my professor responded in kind with a paradox of his own, Pete Sommers would have taken a different path.

Because I was still on the outside, Elias, a.k.a. Pete, had never explained the use of this tool, but instead, he simply appeared to have been acting silly. Eventually, I would also learn to speak in the same fashion. It may sound absurd, but in several weeks, I was about to become a living paradox existing as *the twin sons of different parents*.

Had I been informed about the anomaly of paradoxical communication between IPMers earlier, I very likely would've avoided my eventual kidnapping by Oden Chang, just a few months later, after fleeing to the recesses of Kuala Lumpur. Yes, we're talking about Indonesia! Unbeknownst to me the day the three of us stood in my paleontology class, radical changes were about to consume and transform my existence.

Thinking back with me for a just a moment to my first semester in college. It's difficult to believe I was only 60 or 70 days away from blowing up a sleek, new Mercedes Benz and taking out several evil men in the process who intended to torture me to death. Someone once reflected, "What a long, strange journey it has been!" Only the likes of Levi Martin could have gotten himself into a load of crap like this!

Pete went on to give a mini-lecture on the importance of innovators in the petroleum research community. He had a few things to say about cutting-edge breakthroughs in oil drilling, the experimental technique of fracking, and advances in harnessing geothermal energy.

"In your lifetime, we expect to see water furnaces being used in private residences that extract energy from hundreds of feet below the earth's surface in order to heat and cool your homes. The cost will be far lower than fossil fuels and will decrease our dependence upon petroleum, coal, and natural gas."

He went on a few minutes longer, then concluding his brief speech, he turned to our professor admiringly, "From what I've heard, Dr. Adler runs a well-designed, rigorous course."

The department head nodded graciously at the comment.

Then, Sommers turned his attention to me in front of the class, "I wanted to stop by today to meet you Levi and to congratulate you on your hypotheses and findings. You've taken initiative in the practical application of Dr. Adler's expertise."

Again, my professor smiled, being moved by the open flattery.

"The letters and maps you've prepared for Shilling are being passed up the corporate food chain as we speak. These ideas are being given serious attention by some of our top geologists and business leaders."

I overheard a classmate whisper to another, "Is he really talking about Levi Martin?"

Then, Sommers looked back at Dr. Adler, "Keep up the good work. The industry needs more professionals like yourself who cut through the minutia and lead students on to success."

Sommers crossed the room theatrically cocking his head and reached out to shake my hand. He placed a sealed envelope next to the fossil tray on the table.

"Here's my office number, Levi. Call me when you get some free time to arrange a visit to our New York City facility." Then, he waved at the class, nodded with gratitude at my professor, and departed through the side door.

Little did I realize in that moment that Pete Sommers had just turned the loser, Levi Martin, into a superstar celebrity. For my own part, I was psyched, simply because I finally had Jefferson's contact information.

Axiom Sixty

Mind games can improve your cumulative average.

Based on my test scores, my G.P.A. was probably only a "D+" or at best, a "C-" for the paleontology course. That included additional credit I'd received for my occasional acts of servitude. However, I received a "B" as a final grade. Why? Simple! The professor couldn't afford to give a lower grade to one of his students who was destined for a future with a major oil corporation. There was also more duplicity involved in how I earned that mark, because Pete Sommers' impromptu classroom appearance set a series of deceptive events into motion that made my life pretty intense over the following month.

Word spread fast about Sommers and Schilling Oil throughout the department and even in the academic and business offices. My collegiate social existence changed remarkably in a single day. In the coming weeks, I was treated with a great deal of respect. Even upperclassmen wanted to hang out with me afterward to see if I could hook them up with the oil conglomerate.

The soothing feeling of power and control felt good.

"I'll be glad to tell you everything about getting connected with Shilling." I lied, "Sommers tells me they're likely to hire several New Paltz students between now and next year. How about dinner and I show you the ropes?"

I became well fed at the expense of my new friends for the rest of the semester at the burger and pizza joints downtown.

"Hey, Sebastian! Didn't you say you were interested in finding a job having something to do with coal production?"

"Yeah, Levi, can you give me a lead?"

"Sure thing, I have a few names. What are you doing for dinner tonight?"

After filling up on lasagna and spumoni, I gave Sebastian contact information for three guys that I found in the back of a magazine in Dr. Adler's lab.

"Sommers told me these guys are currently recruiting. Send them a letter of introduction with your transcript. Say you're interested in work-study for your last semester."

I was set like a king, and he invited me to a senior party. Although I alone knew the shallow admiration was completely founded on falsehood, the sudden popularity was intoxicating! I'd never eaten so well in all my life. When we were kids, feasting until we were stuffed almost never happened except at Thanksgiving and Christmas. If Wendell or one of my cousins could only have been there to see and experience it with me!

Alas, it appeared that I'd made a success of the first intellectual challenge I'd signed up for with M.C. Jacob. Where was the difficulty?

Axiom Sixty-One
Discern between a "friend" and a "frenemy."

That weekend, Jacob stopped by. M.C.s ran all the new student gatherings and provided the ongoing challenges for the research of Jefferson's book. They always arrived out of the blue. So long as I didn't have an algebra or chemistry test the next day that I needed to prove I could fail, I was game for another problem-solving adventure.

It was a cold Saturday morning in October and we headed out on a trip. Jacob had me grab a change of clothes.

As we drove, he asked, "So don't tell me you're the geology student named 'Levi' who everyone in administration is talking about."

A surge of excitement went through me. "What? Well, maybe. Tell me more."

Passing through town, I saw the skinny, older guy we called "Mr. Bojangles" standing on Main Street. He wasn't a beggar, but he always looked hungry. I shouted to my chauffer, "Hold on. Stop for a second."

"What the heck, Levi?"

I hopped out and gave the man a $5 bill, telling him, "Get some lunch!" He smiled at me, and I jumped back in the car.

Pastor James' voice lived in my mind. "When you see someone in need, do something about it right then and there."

Having gone to bed hungry more than once myself, I felt the need to take care of the few that I could. Pastor James often gave away the whole church offering to fund the soup kitchen on the edge of town. He taught by example that "Authentic love makes sacrifices to share."

When I was back in the car, we went on with the discussion of today's challenge.

Jacob worked part-time in admissions managing the applications of multilingual students. "Word is spreading in the office about a big-wig oil company executive's visit to a student named 'Levi.' That's not you, is it? I mean you just arrived here."

Having heard my own name in a context of discussion associated with fame, I wanted to shout, "Holy cow, man!" But I stayed calm and acted aloof. "Yeah, sure thing. I'm trying to play it cool though, because I don't want to come off like some wise-ass, big shot."

Since Jacob had invited me into the problem-solving exercises, I was surprised that he didn't know about Dr. J's actions as "Pete Sommers." I later learned that IPM operated on a need-to-know basis, and often, the right hand didn't know what the left was doing. Nevertheless, I'd assumed the M.C. was somehow going to be part of these too. I realized pretty fast that he didn't have any idea what was going on.

I decided to take advantage of Jacob's ignorance and play with him a little. "I shared some ideas I had with Shilling Oil, so they sent a guy up here to offer me a stipend and work-study this summer."

Jacob sounded a little ticked off. "Well, how the heck did you manage that? You're barely even a freshman!"

"Honestly, I didn't think it would amount to much, but I came up with a few ideas about petroleum exploration and passed them along to their research team. I guess they liked it. Nothing special, Jacob. Really!" I observed the look of consternation on his face then added, "This guy Sommers wants to get me down to the city next week for a luncheon to meet some guys and to tour the corporate center. He's arranged a limo."

Jacob looked befuddled and remained silent, as if he couldn't figure out how to respond. His sentiment of displeasure at my good fortune was evident.

I ended the story by bragging about the upcoming senior party and confided in him how I was using the oil man's visit to extort pizza and burgers from my classmates.

I figured that all of this would muster a sense of camaraderie, as would have been the case with any of my cousins. I thought that Jacob would come around to relish in my excitement. Getting to hang out with some of the hoity-toity guys at school was a big deal and I'd expected the M.C to congratulate me. This was not the case.

Jacob made it plain that he was put off by the entire discussion. "Yeah, whatever, Martin. Good luck with all of that." After a pause and with more emotion, he added, "The whole thing is stupid, Levi!"

Clearly, he was finished with our discussion.

Axiom Sixty-Two
When things don't make sense trust your gut.

So, I suppose these days I could look it up on Google Maps. I'm not sure exactly where we drove, but it was near Accord. There's a bridge by a fork in the river with some giant rocks that make a good swimming hole in the summer. However, the weather had changed, and the October wind had driven all the leaves off the trees. Where we stood watching, the frigid water flowed steadily past a small cliff.

Jacob explained, "You need to jump from the bluff into the water and try to take two steps before sinking. Then you need to get out as quickly as possible."

It was probably only a ten to twelve-foot jump and then maybe a twenty-foot swim to shore. There was nothing intimidating about the challenge, except for not freezing my butt off. I wondered, "Why the 'two steps?'"

I stood there quietly analyzing the situation. The M.C. remained silent and observed. In the past, I'd always found a semantic trick of interpretation or an outside-the-box means of completing IPM's challenges. We were standing on a "bluff" and he'd mentioned the term. Did that indicate that Jacob was only "bluffing?"

I racked my brain to consider any alternate means of interpreting his directive. Was there something to a "first step" and a "second step." It must have been so obvious that I couldn't see it.

I recalled how "I'd cut 'MY TIME' in half," with a pair of scissors the previous month. I'd initially interpreted the request narrowly as if it had to do with time and speed, then later, I realized the wordplay double-meaning.

Standing above the cold water, I ventured to ask, "Is there anything else that I need to know?"

Jacob replied flatly, "No."

Even though I considered myself to be a fairly talented problem solver, I was at a loss to find any other overt or hidden significance to the M.C.'s demand. I stopped short of admitting that I was completely stumped and became suspicious.

I risked a candid glance at Jacob and wondered if he might just be messing with me. He appeared to be enjoying my perplexed evaluation of the situation.

After several more moments, Jacob looked at me and said, "So? The water is waiting for you, Levi."

I didn't get anything else from that clue if it was one. He clearly and plainly expected me to jump.

Axiom Sixty-Three
The person who controls the communication
also controls the engagement.

A shift took place in my strategy. I looked back at Jacob decisively, as if I now understood and had psyched myself up for a swim. I removed my watch and put it on the rock with my wallet and rubbed my hands together. I pursed my lips and looked at him affirmatively as I peered theatrically down over the edge.

Then, I subtly motioned with a nod of my head for him to stand next to me to look at something below. Up to this point, Jacob had been calling all the shots, but I silently took control of the engagement.

In order to see what I'd motioned him toward, he moved forward ahead of me on the rock. He glanced back as I slipped off my shoes and removed my shirt.

Jacob noticed my odd expression. Not having seen anything out of the ordinary, he asked, "What?"

I froze and looked back down as if though I was scrutinizing something hiding just beyond the ledge. As I slipped off my jeans, once more, he cautiously edged forward, staring at the water.

There was no obvious reason for my indications, but as he looked back inquisitively, I raised my index finger over my lips signaling him to remain silent. I pointed vigorously downward several more times. As he leaned over further this time in order to see, I became fully in control of Jacob's future. He'd unwittingly become my prey.

I lurched against him, shoving him face first toward the water in a free fall. He spread eagle screaming into the icy current. Jacob's shriek was indelibly seared into my mind and to this day I still find enjoyment reliving the moment.

His splash shattered the serenity of the late golden leaves that had been drifting quietly along the liquid confluence. If there only had been a camera to capture the priceless look of shock on his face as he met with destiny!

When his head resurfaced, the sound of his vulgarity was drowned by the torrent of my laughter. The moral of the story is when you get that certain bad feeling in your gut, go against the flow.

I declared, "A chilling foiled by the prodigy of Shilling!"

Axiom Sixty-Four
Maintain the best ideals of your family legacy.

It's important to understand my background and heritage. There were two sides to my family. There were the Lithuanian Huns who'd bred with the Norse Vikings. They'd either trick you into peeing on the electric fence or openly challenge you to see who could hold his stream steadily spraying on the live wire for the longest amount of time. We were no strangers to trouble or troublemakers.

Not only had my childhood prepared me well for my involvement with IPM, but in this case, it saved me from the jealous antics of Jacob.

Axiom Sixty-Five
The mouth speaks what the heart is full of.

Jacob had shown his cards with his bad attitude. With the realization of the jealous flaw in his character, I'd been empowered to find a means of safe navigation around his evil intent.

It wasn't until my formal training with IPM when I learned that Jacob had heard braggadocios stories about me from Josef. I don't think the two of them got along particularly well, because Josef was chosen over Jacob for a long-term assignment in another country. Josef rubbed Jacob's face in some things, and somehow, I'd become one of those things.

The less mature M.C. had a narcissistic obsession, living with the erroneous notion that few individuals were more clever or deserving than himself. Indeed, Jacob was unparalleled in certain talents. He was one in a million. However, he pridefully let others' compliments go to his head.

He'd arrogantly announced to Josef on several occasions, "Levi Martin is an imbecile! He thinks he's so smart! I don't see why everyone thinks he's so great."

Jacob began to hate everything about me and nitpicked to find fault. He sourly argued, "This is all wrong! If we're considering him as a new M.C., he shouldn't be let off the hook in helping to organize our meetings. He's wasting time going to Bible studies, drinking beer downtown, and shooting pool at Brandus! He needs to start pulling his weight around here!"

A distorted perspective had grown up and taken control

of his mind. Nothing was fair so long as it had to do with good things happening for me. Like a thorn pressing continually tighter into his side, drawing blood, and fostering infection, he became the victim of his own unbalanced thoughts.

Axiom Sixty-Six
Jealousy is a sickness.
Be honest about your jealousy and get help.

My first semester in college, both Josef and Jacob worked for an IPM front known as the "Kingston County Corrections Unit." Fooled into thinking that their efforts served the needs of a local state law enforcement agency overseen by Dr. Elias Jefferson, both were faithful servants. Initially, neither of them had actually ever heard of IPM.

The corporation hired individuals into a series of smaller organizations like KCCU, which were established to implement project designs taking down known criminals. Thinking they were setting up sting operations, gathering and delivering evidence for covert, undercover, state, and federal prosecutions, they were led to believe they were criminal justice interns. After the completion of a project in taking down a known felonious character, IPM used a variety of front organizations to funnel the stolen financial resources of their targets back into their own bank accounts. From a benevolent viewpoint, it might be observed that IPM simply cleaned up the world while getting paid for their work. From a fiduciary, legal perspective, they were engaged in high level theft which made them rich. The company collected untold millions. Whatever shadow of criticism might have been expressed over the latter notion was far outweighed by the good their existence provided for society. In order to accomplish its goals, IPM sidestepped the red tape, legal entanglements, and bureaucracy of the U.S. and worldwide judicial systems to more efficiently make the world a safer place. They took great risks and were rewarded handsomely.

Jacob worked among KCCU leaders, while they celebrated a series of recent successes. What he heard in that time, however, drove him crazy.

"Martin sure made fools of the guys in that chicken outfit!"

"Yeah, and it's changed everything for the better in Seychelles too!"

"Hey! How about his chase with Crazy Joe? Levi was magnificent! The driver said he rode home without a complaint as if it was all in a day's work."

"I heard Joe is now facing 60 years to life on the first set of charges."

"Josef flew the plane packed with cash out of there and delivered it to the feds in New Jersey."

"He couldn't have done it so easy if Levi hadn't led Joe on such a long chase that ended with the target's arrest for carjacking."

"I hope the new guy from California works out. Are you certain he's only a freshman?"

"Yep. At 18 years of age, he's looking pretty darn good so far!"

"I thought he was 19?"

"His birthday isn't until the end of the year."

"He's amazing for a teenager!"

Jacob's inability to appreciate others' successes, who he

wrongly viewed as competition instead of as comrades, pissed him off to the degree that he felt driven to formulate his own plan to make me appear as a fool.

Days earlier, when news flittering through the enrollment office reached his ears that a certain geology student named "Levi" had received accolades from a high-ranking petroleum executive, it was too much. He was pushed over the edge and decided to take matters into his own hands; which of course, literally resulted in getting himself pushed over the edge.

The discussion during our ride out to the river in Accord was more than he could bear. I was innocently unaware of all this until that shivery October morning standing half naked on the bluff. A few thoughts began to add up. Not only had he hoped I'd fail at the escape challenges, he'd counted on it. Nevertheless, by sheer luck, fate, or more likely, the intervention of the Almighty, I advanced.

As he swam to the shore, I threw Jacob the end of the towel to grasp. I let it down to help pull him up out of the water. He was cussing up a wicked storm and a half and yanked the towel from my grip. I was still holding my side laughing as I made the feeble attempt to strap my watch back on my wrist. This was an event fit for preservation in the lore of Martinhood!

As I regained my composure I asked, "So what's this all about, Jacob?"

He muttered angrily, "I was going to test and see if those Bible studies were doing you any good! I wanted to figure out if you could walk on water!"

He kicked up a splash from the shallows, that pooled on the ground between us.

"Walking on water is easy, Jacob. Watch this!"

I stepped into the puddle that was quickly soaking into the river bank.

I chided him further, "You're free to learn some of these things if you join us on Friday nights, but don't assume that we're going to let you in on our secrets all at once!"

He shivered violently as he continued swearing, got into his car, slammed the door, and kicked up gravel when he sped away. I ended up hitch-hiking back to New Paltz.

Apparently, at some point down the road, Jefferson admonished Jacob, "You're better than all this!" After they had several long talks, things began to improve between the two of us.

Axiom Sixty-Seven
When you're in a pinch, buy time.

Dr. Adler ended our next geology class five minutes early and called me into his office. I could tell he'd been thinking. He wanted to know the details of how I gained the attention of someone as prominent as Pete Sommers. It was difficult to control the expression on my face as the instructor proceeded with his interrogation.

"Have a seat, Levi."

"Sure, thank you, sir."

"Mr. Sommers introduced himself and mentioned you commenting, 'Mr. Martin must be one of your most prominent students!' Ha! I decided to keep the controversy of your poor academic status private for the time being, Levi; at least until I understood more about the man's intent. So, enlighten me about all of this, will you please?"

Responding to one question with another is a great way to buy time and investigate a situation.

"I don't want to waste a moment telling you things you already know. If you fill me in with the details of what Sommers told you, I'll pick up from there."

"Okay. Pete Sommers said you'd made several inquiries regarding oil drilling that gained the attention of Shilling's N.Y. City office. He flashed a few letters that you'd written, and I saw some hand-drawn maps with diagrams. He didn't let me read them for myself but commented that you'd 'cinched up some impressive conclusions' regarding 'certain stratigraphic fossil finds that might predict the presence of petroleum resources.' Honestly, Levi, if I hadn't recognized the messy handwriting from your exams, I'd have insisted that Sommers had the wrong student!"

I nodded, said, "Okay," and let him continue.

"I wanted to get a closer look at your notes and held out my hand for the papers, but he explained that his time was short before another appointment."

"I'm sure Levi can tell you about these, but if you have just 5 more minutes, I'd love the opportunity to meet your class to share a few insider comments about Shilling's private innovations and a few emerging developments in the energy industry."

"With that, he stashed your work back into his briefcase."

The way he recounted their meeting indicated that Dr. Adler was miffed about being left out of the loop.

"Apparently you attributed some of your calculations to conclusions I've made in our class. It was nice of you to have passed along the credit, Levi. Now, I'm intrigued, and I want to hear what you found."

I was both astonished by the interchange and thrown off guard by the mention of the series of forged letters. Jefferson or Sommers had gone to great lengths to make this a believable scam. The problematic question of where Dr. J had seen my penmanship and how he'd reduplicated it didn't occur to me until later.

Axiom Sixty-Eight
Flattery of the tongue spreads a net for the feet
~ King Solomon ~

Dr. Adler's countenance brightened for my supposed acknowledgment of his expertise. Pete Sommers' adulation in our classroom had further disarmed my professor of his critical thinking ability so that he'd bought into the whole story.

Dr. J had created an imaginary world in the mind of my professor using an alias with an official title from an industrial conglomerate. His ingenious plan included artifacts to support his claims. It was an enormous lie that the Martins would've been proud of. The character of Sommers had performed brilliantly!

Believing the whole delusion was true, Dr. Adler leaned back in his office chair with folded hands, remarking, "Levi, it's time for *the two of us* to get down to business about how *we're* going to further help Pete Sommers!"

I tried to listen as he went on about the value of these kinds of findings, but my thoughts were suddenly racing. Dr. Adler had upped the ante on the whole ruse with his plural use of the pronoun "we." He wanted in on the deal, and this meant I was going to be forced into contriving a whole new set of lies to sustain the imaginative set of circumstances the Sommers character had set into motion.

I found myself being thrust right into the middle of a giant mind game! Did I have the wherewithal to survive as a star player who existed in the world of make-believe? CRAP! The lie had progressed forward demanding me to live out the identity of a successful, smart student. That wasn't going to be easy! Could Adler hear my heart pounding? I began to panic like a mouse being backed into a corner by a large, hungry tomcat.

I nervously glanced at my watch.

Adler asked, "Do you have to get to another class?"

I lied, "Yeah, but I'd be glad to get together later."

He looked at his planner and asked, "When is good?"

DANG! I wasn't expecting us to set up the appointment right then and there.

"How about Monday? Lunch at the Rat at noon?"

This was our affectionate nickname for the Rathskeller.

"Sure thing, Dr. Adler."

I kicked myself again later that afternoon when I realized how valuable this information probably appeared to my professor. Here I'd settled for a cheap lunch at the Rat! I determined that somehow this would eventually lead to a steak dinner at the tennis club restaurant on the northwest edge of New Paltz.

My upbringing had included inventing all kinds of stories, but this one would require longterm planning, sustained pretense, and fabrication of evidence to support lies. I was being forced onstage as an intelligent person who had something constructive to offer the world. What had I gotten myself into? No wonder Jacob was smiling when I'd agreed to all of this!

Axiom Sixty-Nine
When you figure out the game, get with the game fast.

By assuming that he was already my partner, Adler realized he could force expectations upon me to reveal what I'd allegedly handed off to Sommers. He also controlled my final grade for the semester. By either failing at my act or by not coming up with my own supporting geological notes and props would result in tragic consequences!

I had only one option, which was to play out my role and maintain the facade. It would be a complicated endeavor, inviting my professor into a non-existent world, where he could also become a player at Shilling Oil.

I decided the best thing to do was to call Jefferson to get some suggestions on how I should proceed.

Axiom Seventy
A neatly organized life reduces potential for panic.

I thought I'd put the envelope with Pete Sommers' contact information with my stack of notebooks on my desk. My junk was all mixed up with Brad's in a jumbled-up mess. Our piles had overtaken most of the floor space, and I panicked at first when I couldn't find it. My roommate's pet rat, Beth, was constantly on the loose. She was a hoarder, and I momentarily feared that she'd dragged it off, chewed it up, and used it to build a nest under the bed.

In the recesses of my mind, I once again heard Mom's voice, "You and Wendell get in there and clean that room!"

There it was next to the radiator between the bookshelf and the desk. I opened it and read:

Greetings Levi,

You may wonder what is going on with my visit to your paleontology lab as "Pete Sommers." This is one of the intellectual challenges in problem-solving mentioned to you by Jacob. The test remains for you to use this situation in a way to better your position in the geology course. The only rule is that Dr. Adler can't be allowed to discover the hoax. I know you've got this handled already! Think of this as playing mind games.

DANG! He lied. I turned the envelope inside out, but there wasn't a phone number or address to be found. I was on my own! Pete laid the gauntlet, and he was obviously somewhere off in the distance looking over my shoulder. I felt his invisible presence.

Axiom Seventy-One
Live in the moment. Take one step at a time.

In the second half of my first semester of physical education class, I fell in love with the highly competitive game of racquetball. It was fast, exciting, and there were lots of adrenaline rushes. Infrequently, someone got smashed in the eye or the head with a ball or by a racquet, which wasn't much fun. Nevertheless, I kept going back to the game.

We had a standing deal with our instructor. If you could beat him, he'd give you an "A" in the class. The brave ones signed up on the roster posted on his door for the opportunity to help their transcripts. I can't lay claim to an ounce of courage in my blood, but there have always been several quarts of desperation coursing through my veins. I needed an "A" in the class to raise my overall G.P.A. If Mom didn't see academic improvement, she might demonstrate her assertion that I'd never be too big to be turned over her knee.

My first game with the coach, I determined that I'd slaughter him hard and fast. But, no matter how quick I moved, he outsmarted me. He was much slower, yet always found himself in a better position. As I recall, I scored only a few points in the game. He took me apart with a smile on his face. With glinting eyes, he shook my hand as we left the court. I heaved for breath in exhaustion, but he hadn't even broken a sweat.

Back in the 80s, smoking was still permissible inside, and the funny thing was that toward the end of the game, I could smell the distinct fragrance of cherry tobacco wafting through the air. The upper third of the back wall of the court was open to the hall above. It allowed onlookers to watch matches, but also let the strong cherry scent into the court. Suspecting that Dr. Jefferson, a.k.a. "Pete Sommers," was nearby, I bounded up the stairs in time to find him leaning against the wall by the open door. He seemed to know that I'd track him down.

He asked, "Do you know why you lost the game, Levi?"

I replied, "No." But then, I admitted with resolve, "The coach is just a better player."

Dr. J agreed, "That might be the case, Levi. After all, your instructor did write a book on the game." He paid me a small compliment, "You're very fast, Levi." But then, he also offered some corrective advice, "You were in an arena where speed might offer a few good saves, but you need more than that to win."

I listened.

"You played like you were planning on beating him the moment you entered the arena, right?"

I nodded affirmatively and added, "I was gonna' demolish him in front of the whole class!"

I'd gone in there with an overconfident attitude, proud, and feeling strong, but I proved something else by my performance.

Dr. Jefferson offered some sage advice, "Next time you play the coach, proceed just hoping to get a single point. If you score, continue playing just hoping to get a second point and so on."

Realizing there might only be a few more limited opportunities for a rematch with the instructor, I went in the next week to sign up outside his door. Looking at the schedule, I was surprised at what I saw. There, before Thanksgiving break, was my name already sloppily spelled out on the roster! When had I done that? I couldn't recall signing up after our match the week before, but then again, maybe I had. I examined the paper closely, and it was definitely my own handwriting. Was I going crazy?

Axiom Seventy-Two
Winning is the result of going for each point individually and remaining steady.

Later, when the date of our rematch arrived, I followed Dr. J's advice. As my score grew larger, a crowd of onlookers began to gather behind us in the overhead hallway. The balcony overlooking our court was crowded. The number of spectators increased as my score inched upward and was about equal with that of the coach. As the game progressed, I finally advanced several points ahead. By that time, nearly the entire class, who weren't playing in other matches, were crammed together watching.

I heard wagering going on, up above behind us. Money was changing hands. I kept playing hard, but just for each point. I remained calculated. Eventually, I needed just one more point. I returned the coach's serve. He hit it squarely rebounding the ball low to the far side of the court. I made a great dash to the ball and clipped it up to the wall a split second before it would've hit the floor. The coach was unable to maneuver back around, and his racquet remained out of reach. The ball bounced twice and rolled forward from the back wall. Unbelievably, I'd scored the winning point!

The coach objected that I didn't hit the ball in time and had let it touch the ground. Several students watching from above disagreed in unison. It had been a fair shot.

Amidst the discussion between the other students, the coach, and the settling of the gambling arrangements, I became aware of the fact that once again the unmistakable fragrance of cherry tobacco wafted in from the hall. I shook hands with the coach, thanked him for the rematch, and I rushed out of the little door at the back of the court. I dashed up the stairs. Man, oh man, if I was ever ready for a pat on the back, it was then. I looked everywhere for Dr. Jefferson, but strangely, he was nowhere to be found. Nevertheless, the cherry aroma filling the air spoke volumes. Through his silent absence, Dr. Jefferson demonstrated, once again, that he remained in control of the engagement. Although there was much to admire about Dr. J, he was getting under my skin.

Axiom Seventy-Three
Chew your food slowly.
Disclose information in the same manner.

When I met with Dr. Adler for lunch at the Rat, I ordered this giant meatball sub, two slices of pizza, an order of fries, cheesecake, cookies, and a large Dr. Pepper. I was going for broke just in case we never made it out to the tennis club for a steak dinner. The other part of my strategy was to get such a huge quantity of food that I wouldn't have much time for questions. I ate slowly and kept my mouth full of food.

He began by taking out a pencil and paper and slid them across the table to me. "Levi, I need to know that I'm not wasting my time."

Between mouthfuls, I mumbled, "Okay."

"If I ask you to draw a diagram of the stratigraphic layers spanning the width of the United States with the oil finds beneath them, can you do that? Pete Sommers implied that you were knowledgeable about this."

Holy cow! There were more than a hundred layers in Poughkeepsie, N.Y. alone! A cross-section of the entire country was a Ph.D. level exercise. I almost choked on a meatball!

Axiom Seventy-Four
Bluff big like you mean it.

I swallowed hard, thought for a second, and then wondered if I might find a way of turning my situation around.

I asked, "Okay, should I draw the cross-section of the layers that span the northern United States or the southern strata?"

Dr. Adler had this look of marvel on his face and retorted, "You can really do both?"

I jumped in fast and interrupted his momentary pause before he had time to choose. "Listen, we can waste the next two hours doing this exercise or we can just get to the point of the fossil finds and the location of the oil."

Thank heaven that he liked the second idea better!

For the next thirty minutes, I spoke in circles regarding sedimentary layers in the U.S. that contained different fossils. This information came straight off a chart from our textbook. It was the same source from which I'd derived a list of the major continental oil resources. The single added component that I fabricated was the supposition that there was a matching angularity of the sediment deposits resting over the petroleum reserves.

I explained, "The main point of my correspondences with Shilling concerned a commonality in the kinds of fossils found in the strata and the direction of the tilt in the layers."

I seemed to have hit pay dirt in Dr. Adler's mind. "Really? That's quite fascinating."

I rolled with it, "Yeah, I put together a few charts based upon the stratigraphy maps with some speculation that certain fossils pointing in one direction or another might predict energy resources below. It might either be oil, natural gas or coal." I continued lying like my life depended on it, "I've spent more hours in the library than I can count."

"Okay, then, we have to take a closer look at all this."

"Yeah, well, that's going to be a problem because I sent all my charts, maps, and notes I'd made on this stuff to Shilling Oil. They'll get back to me soon again though, don't you think?"

Like a good listener, he didn't miss a beat. I interpreted a sense of fatalism in his change of expression and intonation. He lamented, "Well, Levi, I don't think that's going to happen. What you've stumbled upon could be worth a great deal of money. The fewer people who know about it, the more valuable it might be."

I realized I was out of things to say and glanced at my watch with concern. Dr. Adler inferred the message that I had to leave soon.

"Another class to get to?"

"Yes, sir," I replied.

"It's going to take some time to reduplicate the drawings and notes I sent off to Schilling. How about I do what I can, and then, we meet for dinner at the tennis club restaurant Friday evening?"

I hoped he'd go for it and added, "My roommate works there and serves up an amusing tableside flambé Gila Monster. He makes it using a carved cucumber with a forked carrot tongue."

Adler went for the bait, but I was even more psyched because the tables had turned. Instead of him using me to set up any more of his staff meetings in exchange for a few points added to my exams, I'd eat like a king on his credit card.

Axiom Seventy-Five
Study your adversary.
Understand the limitations of the playing field.

One of the challenges presented by an M.C. was to engage the campus security and then to elude them in a challenge known as the "Forty Minute Chase." He warned us, "Only an idiot will attempt this in a car. You have to plan this to take place on foot."

By this point in life, I thought I'd shaken myself free from some of the bright ideas that characterized my younger days. However, the next several weeks ahead proved I was wrong. Even though Mom had frequently threatened to tear my arm off and beat me to death with the bloody limb, I'd somehow miraculously managed to make it to college standing in Mom's shadow with both arms still intact. Nevertheless, all of my successes with the coach, Adler, and even in this chase weren't going to be enough to save my butt from landing in a Thai prison cell in about 30 or 40 days.

There were typically three officers or so on duty in the campus security detail. One of them usually remained in the office acting as a dispatcher. Two of them either drove around separately or in the same vehicle. There weren't any direct routes across campus, and the road, more or less, curved around the perimeter. Lots of stairways, uneven terrain, and a waterway with footbridges separated most of the dorms and cafeteria from the library, faculty, administration, and classroom buildings. Located at the far western side of the premises was the Old Main building and the rest of the original college. A person in a car was set at a disadvantage if he attempted to chase someone on foot, that is unless he found you out in the sports fields or someplace exposed in the wide open. If you stayed between the buildings and always moved perpendicular to the roads you could succeed at eluding the authorities.

Our challenge was to escape after 40 minutes of chase. Figuring that the game of cat and mouse was going to be fun and realizing that there were advantages which could be used in the terrain, I saw no reason I wouldn't be successful. In the end, however, we escaped only because we were extremely lucky; having encountered a great deal more than we bargained for.

I enlisted my adventure seeking roommate, Brad, into the project. He never had any idea that what we were really doing was a part of the research for Dr. J's book.

Brad was an adventurous, cool guy. His Dad worked for a telecommunications conglomerate in Rhode Island, and they had a phone in every room of the house; even in the bathrooms. So, what was totally outstanding was that we also had a private line in our room. Because it was sometimes difficult to locate ours, due to the mess, I still mostly used the payphone in the hall.

Brad tended to pile all of his belongings in heaps. Clothes, books, papers, and sports equipment often rose from the top of his desk all the way to the upper shelf in his closet. Mom never would have believed that anyone was sloppier than me or Wendell. To make matters worse, his pet rat, named "Beth," would get out and be on the lamb for days. In the night, she'd empty our cereal boxes and make nests with stolen items she'd scavenged from the room. Often enough, whenever she got loose, the rodent enjoyed gnawing through the phone cord.

134

Before the rat, we had a noisy hamster that we inherited from Brad's girlfriend. It kept us up all night digging in his cage and running on the squeaky wheel. "Scratcher," as he was aptly named, eventually passed due to an overdose of cold medicine he was experimenting with as a nighttime sedative.

Brad could have stood on his own amongst the Martin Clan. Time and again, he practiced making new kinds of explosive devices. After Thanksgiving vacation, I'd brought back a large box of fireworks, and he almost got us evicted by shooting a skyrocket out our window at a campus security car. My parents definitely wouldn't have been happy had they gotten news of my expulsion from college! We were only saved, because the police never got an exact fix on the location of its origination. They sat outside and watched our dorm for an hour. If they'd opted for a foot search, going from room to room, they'd have easily identified our suite as the source from the horrible burnt sulfur smell of the rocket exhaust.

Axiom Seventy-Six
Successful people plan to succeed.

I was glad that Brad was up for the game when I asked him about joining me in the Forty Minute Chase. He had no idea what I was really up to.

In preparation, I thought I'd done a terrific job figuring out the logistical limitations for traversing the campus in order to avoid the security detail. I formulated a plan giving us a lengthy stint on the run with a deceptive escape route. What I hadn't counted on was that the limited SUNY police were going to call in reinforcements.

The Lecture Center was connected by pedestrian tubes between the Humanities Classroom Building and the Library. The architecture of the Lecture Center had walls made up of large plate glass with venting awning windows at the bottom. These were mostly hidden from the exterior view by low lying shrubs. Someone hiding behind those bushes could climb through the window if it was unlocked and then crawl across the lobby floor without being seen. These architectural and landscaping features were going to allow us to disappear without a trace at the end of our jaunt.

Engaging the security team wasn't difficult. We just waited until after dark and let them catch us in their headlights. Then, we ran as if we were guilty of something. The pursuit was on, and the clock was running!

We cut through buildings, melted into the shadows, and watched our pursuers from here and there. For a while, as we hid behind hedges, dodged around walls, ran up and down stairways, and laid on the ground behind bushes and statues, the security detail didn't even come close to catching us. We darted out and ran to new locations that weren't so easily accessible by car. When we ascended the stairs by the science building, they had to drive all the way around the campus. The whimsical getaway went on and on for half an hour. We continually outmaneuvered our pursuers, constantly using the changes in terrain to our advantage. Looking back now, I think we invented Les Par Cor right then and there. I recall feeling so smug!

The *pièce de résistance* and the mind-bending illusion of our complete disappearance lay just ahead. Shortly before the building closed, at 4:45 p.m., I double checked the locks to be certain the handle latches were opened on the inside.

We let the patrol car catch up a little, and they chased us from the Humanities Classroom Building. Then, we jumped behind the Lecture Center bushes. I estimated that in their perspective, they now had us just about trapped. Before they could get a fix on us, however, we swung the window open, rolled inside, and scurried away in the dark, crawling low across the floor.

One of the security officers sat in the car shining the spotlight while the other frantically searched the bushes with his flashlight. It was obvious they were befuddled as to how we'd escaped. We watched them drive away, shining their lights in every direction. Finally, as they moved ahead and out of sight, I checked my watch. Forty minutes were up. I felt like a ninja who had vanished into thin air! My cousins would've been astonished!

We thought we were done running for the night. It felt good to have won the contest. What we didn't realize was that we were about to walk into a trap.

Axiom Seventy-Seven
Consider ahead of time what your adversary's plan "B" looks like.

Brad and I wandered around inside the Lecture Center Building for a while to warm down. As we exited the lower level on the southern edge of the campus, things got exciting and perhaps a little nerve-racking.

There was only one rule in the Forty Minute Chase: "Whatever happens, don't get caught!"

We walked to the street and noticed two New Paltz Police vehicles circling around the campus. We didn't think anything of them because we were on the perimeter of the adjoining village neighborhood. They were probably on a casual patrol.

We headed in the direction of the Old Main Building and then we realized that the cops were turning around. The spotlight next to the driver's side rearview mirror beamed on us from down the road, so we began running and tore our way up the stairway that looped around the east side of Old Main. They'd have to chase us on foot if they had any hopes of catching us. The front lobby entrance was open, and we ran inside. We started checking a few doors, but all of the offices and classrooms were locked. We huffed our way down to the far west end of the main hall to the foyer of the auditorium.

Brad said, "Hey, what about the catwalk above the stage?"

We quickly discussed hiding up there, but the lights, staging, and curtains wouldn't give us much cover.

I realized aloud, "If they catch us up there, we'll be trapped."

Our time for decision was nearly up. Brad grabbed the doorknob for the closet under the stairs to the left side of the foyer, and it opened.

He motioned and whispered, "Quick, get in here!"

There was no time to argue, because we could hear the outside door opening from just down the hall. Campus security had arrived with the police from the village.

So, with no other choice, we ducked into the trapezoid shaped door. I didn't like the aspect of being cornered. Still, though, I didn't panic because we weren't actually guilty of wrongdoing. We had figured that we could hold out in the building for a while. I turned the latch on the inside of the door to the locked position.

That's when we realized we weren't simply attempting to elude human beings. The unmistakable whine of a dog, and the chinking of a leash and tags was moving down the hall in our direction. They stopped just outside the closet, and the dog began barking and pawing at the door.

A deep serious voice said, "Come out slowly with your hands where we can see them."

Axiom Seventy-Eight
When trapped, remain calm.
Think of a new plan.

IPM's tremendous success was often rooted in the fact that its targets acted impulsively while under pressure. Ones who thought they were trapped frequently either surrendered prematurely or resorted to reactionary brute force and direct opposition. This tactic often led to fatal last stands, like that of Butch Cassidy and the Sundance Kid. Rarely, did they take time to figure a calculated way out of their predicaments.

Later, in formal IPM training, I'd learn that bolting when cornered was often a demonstration of strategic weakness. Rather than resorting to direct confrontation and going to open war against one's adversary, it was better to first conjure an alibi; at least until you had escape options or gained a tactical advantage.

The part of the brain that manages stress is highly volatile. It easily becomes overstimulated by at risk, time-sensitive feelings, or the perception of imminent doom. These dynamics, whether real or imagined, place higher demands on other cerebral processes. The pressure consumes mental energy, and individuals cease to consider other viable options to their perceived dilemmas.

As the mind is overcome with a sensation of agitation, the quarry raise their voices, make counterthreats, lash out, and become reckless. Eventually, they give in to hopelessness, do something stupid, and invite defeat.

Often, an IPM operative who was working a target would make time-critical comments like, "You need to come up with a solution, right now! You're running out of time!" These suggestions facilitated the self-destructive idea that prey had backed themselves into a corner and multiplied their emotional fatigue; further helping to trigger downward spirals toward defeat.

Axiom Seventy-Nine
When things are going good, pray like you mean it.
When things are going bad, pray like you mean it.
The Almighty is a worker of miracles.

As we huddled in the closet, listening to the threats of the tough cop with the deep voice on the other side of the door, my heart was beating out of control. The light wasn't working. Up, down, up, down; I nervously toggled the switch repeatedly, but it remained dark. Worry began to get the better part of me. I wondered if we could sell the police on the story that we thought the boogieman was after us (this was long before zombies achieved their present level of urban legend popularity).

Here is where Brad and I became unbelievably lucky. Anyone who doubts what I say next can go back to the building and verify exactly how we escaped.

As I flipped the switch, oddly enough, a sliver of faint glow lit up and illuminated the perimeter of the floor around us. I was astonished! There must have been an opening beneath the plywood. We crouched to the side and lifted the board on which we'd been standing to find that a rough hole was jack-hammered through the concrete.

I slid down in first. It turned out to be a giant crawl space with a passage leading underneath the seating area of the entire auditorium. There was probably 3' or 4' of headroom. The entire sloping part of the theater above was supported by a vast series of rusty steel I-beams.

We moved further ahead but could still faintly hear the dog barking. The cops were messing with the lock, shouting muffled instructions, "We know you're in there. Don't make us kick the door in!"

I hoped that their plan would include laying siege to the closet for at least another thirty minutes to buy us more time.

Have you ever been chased by the police? Pause here to understand the feeling of pure adrenaline coursing through your veins! It's amazing to think that there's a gland containing something so powerful. My mind and body became a delirious flood of fear, flashing thoughts, and raw energy. In later years, I was chased on several occasions by numerous duplicitous personalities, law enforcement officials, and even a few military personnel. My experience at New Paltz was good practice and nothing at all by comparison to any of those later experiences.

141

Brad and I scrambled ahead toward a dimly illuminated half door on the far wall, which was probably located somewhere beneath the stage. We could no longer hear any of the commotion in the hallway far behind and above us. Thankfully, we were able to open the small door because it had been locked from the other side. We were free to move outward. It led to a large storage room filled with landscaping equipment. Another door exited the rear of the building.

Because of the dog, we didn't want to leave a direct trail back to our dorm, so we ran as hard and fast as we could down into the village. There we called a cab that took us back up to LeFevre Hall.

I was lucky to have such an adventurous roommate who enjoyed messing with authority. Figuring that in the next year or so he would read about the escape in a copy of Dr. J's book, I hadn't let him in on the actual reason for the adventure.

Brad and I had some good times together. We proved that night that we were overachievers and pretty darn lucky!

Axiom Eighty
When you're backed into a corner,
respond with questions that create diversions.

Friday night arrived quickly. As Dr. Adler and I sat down for dinner, I asked, "You commented previously that this could be beneficial for both of us. What did you mean?" It was important to get my end of the bargain sealed as soon as possible.

I appreciated that he was straight to the point, except for the fact that I was trying to drag out our conversation to use up time.

"Well, let's face it, Levi, your test results don't prove that you're an exceptional student. However, I'm willing to accept the fact that some students don't perform well under the duress of typical standardized testing."

I wished I'd thought of that statement whenever the topic of grades came up in the past with my parents.

He continued, "You've managed to convince a leading businessman from an oil conglomerate to personally visit my classroom, which may, in fact, change the way I'm presently thinking about you and your final grade."

I thought to myself, "So then here we are in a situation of extortion." Even so, I was equally guilty, as I thumbed through the menu which didn't even have prices listed. Boy, that steak smelled good. I ordered the double filet mignon, loaded baked potato, salad, and vegetables. After all, if I messed up and he figured out what was really going on, this might prove to be my last meal in New Paltz.

While delving into the *hors-d'oeuvres* assortment, I replied. "Some of us weren't cut out for bookwork and the rigors of the traditional classroom. I'm more of an explorer. Set me loose in a library and I'll disappear behind all the resources." I wanted to add, "...and out the back door." Instead, I continued, "I begin with the endgame and work backward toward solutions. I wind up taking lots of rabbit trails, but I keep learning neat stuff along the way. So, today, in geology, the goal includes finding oil, harnessing geothermal energy, blah, blah, blah, blah, blah, blah, blah..."

I went on and on *ad infinitum* and was glad he was drinking wine. Adler turned out to be a real guzzler, consuming copious amounts of vintage port and becoming more jovial and talkative by the minute. By the time my friend joined us tableside to perform the flambé, my professor was completely wasted. I drove us home in his car. He wasn't going to remember much, but I left a couple sheets of paper on his front seat showing where oil reserves were situated under different kinds of sediments. As if it were a key component of my research, I offered some indication of the tilting direction of the rock layers. I figured I could test what he recalled the next week after class.

Axiom Eighty-One
Intellectual leverage gives its operator dynamic, motivational advantages.

Everybody in the world is controlled by a set of thoughts, values, beliefs, propositions, hopes, and dreams. The human brain has a safety zone that works like a big fence. It provides a feeling of security for the thinker who finds his dwelling within its confines. If an individual is forced outside that mental boundary, commonly referred to as a "comfort zone," he is destabilized and, predictably, will seek to restore order to his world. So long as that remains impossible, he becomes increasingly vulnerable and subject to exploitation.

When people feel as if they're leveraged out of control, they'll often go to desperate lengths to fix their situations. Wait till you eventually hear the story of the power mogul, Angelo Gustav, who burned down his own house, because IPM helped him become convinced that it was haunted! I'm itching to tell it now, but it's in the next book.

I learned in IPM's training that the stronger a person's convictions, the more likely he will fight if he finds himself at a point of instability. The desire to remain in control of one's circumstances is normal. For strong-minded, powerful, influential individuals, it is essential to maintain the predictability of their worlds. In the extreme cases of drug lords, corrupt politicians, merciless dictators, and the kinds of individuals who'd expended vast amounts of money, established sustained lives of deception, and murdered others to become important, it was totally consuming. Since deplorable kinds of characters had worked so hard to get where they were, even the slightest perceived threat to their monetary, social, physical, religious, or cultural acquisitions elicited warlike responses. Perceived threats to their sources of security created pressure that inevitably led to volatility, reaction, and explosive behavior.

When it came to the destruction of wicked empires, IPM's operatives pulled out all the stops, spared no expense, and fought to the death. Nevertheless, their most effective outcomes were usually based on very simple project designs involving between five and eight subtly deceptive steps. Often, that's all it took to undo the most cunning and powerful individuals on the planet. In the criminal world, usually by the sixth or seventh intellectual assault, victims found themselves in unrecoverable spirals toward destruction.

IPM used similar strategies when testing potential recruits, however, these were only one or two steps by design. They weren't trying to ruin anyone's life, just pushing them a few paces beyond the brink of their knowledge, maturity and resources. They were tested and retested in challenges with increasing levels of difficulty. The fittest, luckiest, and most fortunate survived. I chalk my endurance and longevity up to my own stupidity and the merciful beneficence of the Almighty.

As a carefree, fun-loving college kid, I was facing what was known as a "Level 2 FDT" which stood for "Forced Decision Test." That meant the challenge would either include two interventions from an IPM operative, creating a compound problem or a single intellectual assault, presumably, requiring far more endurance and resourcefulness to resolve.

In the deception of Dr. Adler, Pete Sommers' visit to the paleontology lab counted as a single intervention. It forced me outside of my usual laid-back, "Hakuna Matata," lackadaisical attitude; underscored in Disney's movie "The Lion King." Many guys of my age and mentality tended to proceed through life without a plan. The FDTs were intellectual games forcing targets into fight or flight contests, thereby proving survival of the fittest. The stakes were real, and the risks were high. If Adler somehow discovered the whole Shilling Oil ruse was a fraud, I'd have been thrown out of college on my ear. Darwin would have loved this!

In my experience with Adler, I'd gone from being carefree to fearful and then was driven to anger. Every FDT was designed according to criteria to impose problems that would evoke these kinds of emotions. In more advanced tests, the Sommers figure might show up a second time in the professor's office and undermine the recruit's attempted solution, thereby, placing him or her in a catch-22 situation. Operatives were always at risk for betrayal from threats without or within. Low level collegiate practice runs made way for lifesaving endurance in the real world when the stakes were higher.

For a while that first week, I got fat eating food downtown purchased by everyone sucking up to me. Eventually, however, I realized the requirements that were placed upon me to perform. I gained perspective on the scope of the problem and began to fear that I wouldn't be able to get myself out of the jam without making huge mistakes and exposing the entire ordeal for the sham that it really was.

Before long, I realized I needed an exit plan that would shift my situation from that of desperation back to one of control. The more I thought about my predicament the madder I became. IPM needed empirical evidence that a potential recruit was able to manage high-level frustration and still think clearly enough to order a logical set of steps to restore his life. IPM's evil plan was working, testing the hutzpah of Levi Martin.

I realized I wasn't going to be able to count on Adler's inebriation at the tennis club for too many more Friday nights. A few weeks of lobster and steak had increased my waistline, but soon my professor would tire of listening to his own voice.

As an aside, I should mention that we were so poor growing up that we'd often put mustard on our oatmeal because it was all that we had. Wendell and I learned to enjoy that, and if we had any, we'd add pickles on it. Kathy said it was gross, and that was good because it meant there was more for us. On a few occasions Mom took us out for a hamburger at the local fast food place and we ate it with water. We were never so excited and grateful for any meal in our lives. It gave us bragging rights with our cousins. So now, for me to realize I was eating the finest delicacies known to man was mind boggling. I still love what I call "oatslaw" to this very day and add eggs and avocado. My family all agree that it's disgusting, but what do they know without trying it?

One means of resolve for the challenges Jefferson gave me that he probably hadn't counted on was the intervention of the Almighty. I began to pray, calling upon the Lord desperately. As I thought things over, I wondered what kind of deal I'd have to strike with the man upstairs to get me out of this one.

Finally, I promised with all the sincerity in my heart, "Dear Lord, I'm not too keen on my ability to keep my promise to become a missionary to Africa. I really need you to get me out of this, but I can only promise something I really think I'll follow through with. So, I'd go so far as sending in the $25 donation to the radio program Mom used to like, and I'd join their Bible correspondence class. If you could just help me locate a set of findings that would both satisfy Dr. Adler and provide an adequate case study for Dr. Jefferson's book, I'll keep my end of the deal. Amen!"

Whereas the missionary pledge to Africa could pretty much only be resolved in one very costly way, the latter gamble was a safer bet.

I sensed the Almighty answer, "Okay."

That bothered me a little because I'd often answered Mom with an "Okay," but only because the response could imply agreement, while actually simply acknowledging that I'd heard what she said. It was one of those adolescent, rhetorical strategies, sort of like but not quite being a full-fledged lie. "Okays" were useful for getting around the rules and subverting authority. When I sensed the Almighty respond saying, "Okay," I feared he might be messing with me as poetic justice for the way I used to treat Mom.

Axiom Eighty-Two

Do whatever is necessary to master strategies for learning.

A big part of the problem for me at college was that I had no discipline for academic study. Similar to Wendell's trick moves with Ducco, I was pretty good at practical, hands-on training. I'd learned how to climb and suspend myself in the air for nearly an hour using between two and four fixed pressure points with the skill known of as "chimneying." I'd also mastered tying 16 different kinds of knots during Base Camp training in the stifling heat the summer before high school.

It wasn't the same, however, when it came to taking notes from lectures and reading. I didn't feel confident about using books, maps, and other resources the morning I dragged my self-pitying butt into the SUNY, New Paltz Library.

"Excuse me, ma'am, do you have any stratigraphic maps?"

The librarian led me to a large metal cabinet with about 30 drawers that included laminated sets of every kind of map imaginable. I began rummaging through them and spreading them on tables in the back. I very quickly became overwhelmed. Everything I'd shared with Adler came mainly from charts in our textbooks stacked together with the load of crap speculation Sommers and I had given him about my supposed realization of sloping sedimentary layers. I became increasingly stressed because my professor was going to expect more very soon, and it better be something significant that included documented evidence. So far, the hoax was only sustained largely due to Adler's drinking habit, pride, and greed. He'd remain in pursuit only so long as he figured my findings could lead him to notoriety and money.

Axiom Eighty-Three
Growth is healthy.
Forced growth can be frightening.

I found myself being leveraged and I didn't like it. I felt insecure and uncomfortable. It was getting to the point where I'd realized that Dr. J, Pete, or whoever he really was had done a good job of making my life difficult.

I felt exasperated and exhausted the second time I pulled out the maps. Then, I got lucky. I overlaid a stratigraphic map of the United States with one showing the location of prominent oil finds. There were a few overlapping shaded areas between fossils and reserves. Hope at last! This exhausting game of intrigue and darn book of Pete's had better make me famous and provide substantial royalties! It looked like I might be able to fabricate a plausible solution and end up becoming a Bible correspondence student after all!

Axiom Eighty-Four
Plan as much as possible and make calculated decisions.

While at the library, I realized the tremendous value of a large set of green hardbound encyclopedias entitled, "The World Abstract of Commerce and Trade." I could use these to find the numbers for local offices for a variety of oil companies.

I made several phone calls, which in those days cost a fortune in pocket change. I was about $15 into the investigation, when I finally found a geologist at Shilling Oil, of all places, who was willing to talk.

I explained truthfully, "Thanks for your time today sir. I'm a first-semester geology student at SUNY, New Paltz. I'm doing research and hoped a professional in the field might offer a bit of assistance."

It was a relief to hear, "Sure! Shoot!"

"Are there any kinds of patterns with respect to the fossils that are prominently located above oil fields, natural gas reserves, or coal beds?"

"That's a good question. Most strata beds containing fossils are situated in limestone and these all have different variations of organic remnants. Some might have more of one type and less of others."

"Cool."

"Something to consider in your examination might also be 'salacious oozes.'"

"I've never heard of those."

"They're found in deserts, under the oceans, and are comprised of microscopic fossilized debris. They're fascinating to examine under a microscope."

He went on, "As to the correspondence of any of these being systematically located above oil, gas, or coal, I've never heard of anything like that. The strata are too unpredictable."

I jotted down a few notes and thanked him. He also listed several states, where the most recent oil finds were occurring. This was super valuable because that information superseded what was available on the somewhat outdated maps.

If I could just make it appear that I'd found a recurring pattern matching the direction of the layered sloping sediments with the presence of particular fossil types corresponding to energy resources buried in a lower level, I'd have something I could pawn to Adler in exchange for a passing grade. Therein, I'd also be able to provide Dr. Jefferson with a case study for his book.

Finally, I had it: three instances of trilobites found in north sloping strata above oil, five instances of brachiopods in south sloping strata above coal and four salacious oozes blanketing natural gas. In the third instance, the layers of microscopic fossil debris didn't have measurable angularity, but it seemed like a complete enough package to work. Of course, none of this amounted to authentic research. Really, it was just a mixed-up cache of mumbo-jumbo with the appearance of common patterns; a duplicitous operation of reverse engineering. The next challenge would be selling the hoax as a ground-breaking discovery.

I prayed, "Okay, Lord. We're halfway there. Now, please just let this work out with Adler and Jefferson and I'll study the Bible, until I have something valuable to say about it."

Again, I remained wary of his acknowledgment, as I sensed him say, "Okay, Levi."

Why did he have to put it that way?

Axiom Eighty-Five
The fittest survive by being prepared.

I was grinding my teeth as I attempted to re-draw some illustrations I found in the library books and was so consumed with the production that I completely forgot about my Algebra and Chemistry classes that afternoon. Once I got going on a project like this, I could go for hours without sleep or food to get it across the finish line. I had to have something convincing prepared to show Adler.

The exercise didn't prove to be quite so difficult as I'd feared, so I sensed some relief with its completion saying, "Thank you, Lord!" I put down my pen and called the bank to see if I had enough in checking to cover the $25 donation.

Axiom Eighty-Six
Listen for the voice of the Almighty.

I couldn't believe it, but late that night Psycho-Joe showed up outside my dorm. I happened to be walking to the cafeteria when he spotted me and called out.

"You thought you beat me, but I'm gonna' kill you now, Levi Martin!"

I realized this time there wasn't a plan with a car and driver to whisk me away. How did he find me? Where did he get my name? Wasn't he supposed to be in prison? I began running across the campus, over the footbridge, into the lower level of the SUB, up the elevator, out the second level west exit, up two steep sets of stairs, through the art building, traversing the lawn in front of Bouton Hall into the original campus area toward the staircase alongside Old Main.

By the time I was halfway there, it felt as if my feet were stuck in molasses. Psycho Joe had gained on me considerably.

He hollered, "You're not getting out of this alive, Levi Martin!"

I hoped that door to the foyer closet was still unlocked at the front of the auditorium. Maybe I could escape under the stage.

There were loads of people in front of the building surrounding a group of important looking dignitaries exiting a black limousine. Their jewelry glinted in the late afternoon sun. At

153

the same instant I recognized them, they also began pointing at me and formed a line to block my entrance into Old Main. Then, from the east, a detail from the campus security with several New Paltz police officers were running my way; holding a German Shepherd at bay.

I began screaming, "I'm trapped! I'm trapped;" until my voice turned to squawking and the sky began to rain yellow feathers that coated my body. Then, I took on the form of an oversized, bright yellow chicken.

Something hit me in the face as Brad biffed me with his pillow. "Wake up, Levi!" I was jarred back to consciousness, still screaming, and wondered for a moment where I was. I heard Brad's voice in the dark, "You're having one hell of a nightmare bro. I figured I better wake you up before the rest of the guys in the suite think I'm killing you!"

My heart was beating a million miles a minute. Holy cow, that was so stinking real, I couldn't believe it. I'd suffered for nearly five years from nightmares regarding my supposed assassinations of several German, Nazi political leaders, but this was much worse. Now, I was the target. As I tried to calm myself down, I began to think more about the escapes I'd performed for Jefferson. Those guys were really out to get me, and it couldn't have been because of some stupid pranks. What was going on?

That was the first moment that I'd ever had any inkling of a doubt regarding Dr. Jefferson's motives and the authenticity of his claims about a book.

Pastor James used to say, "God will speak to you with dreams, visions, and his still small voice, but only if you have ears to hear and are willing to listen."

154

I wondered, "Is this the Almighty directing my path?"

The more I thought about it, I came to think of myself as a puppet dangling from Dr. Jefferson's strings. Who was he really? I mean this whole thing seemed to have something more to it than research for a stupid book! In the chase by Psycho-Joe, I'd nearly been run over. Just like in the nightmare, he'd have killed me if he'd caught me!

As I completed the finishing touches on the artifacts for Dr. Adler, I felt compelled to find a way to turn the tables on Dr. Jefferson. I wasn't his enemy, but I needed to know more about who he was and what he was really up to.

I'd concluded that he was definitely holding out on me. Why had I given up earlier trying to find his address and additional information about who he was? There had to be more to all of this. The thought came to me that if I could pull down on the puppet master's strings with enough force, I could also gain control of him. What kind of power would that take? How could I use the momentum of another person's control over me for my own advantage?

Axiom Eighty-Seven
Fight fire with fire.

To turn the tables, I decided to examine Dr. J's cadre of tools and equip myself similarly. He had an income, which allowed him to travel into the New Paltz area. I hadn't been able to locate his existence locally. I called Columbia University and spoke with a representative of their alumni association, and somehow, it didn't surprise me when I discovered that "Elias Jefferson" hadn't existed as a student in their academic history. So, the guy was also adept at getting fake documents and inventing new identities.

I became determined about imitating these two primary facets of his life.

If I was going to spy out who he was and what he really did for a living, it made sense to me to copy his resources.

I remembered Durlong's admonishment, "Money is power. Lots of money is lots of power." Although he harped on keeping lots of cash on hand in case of emergencies, he hadn't advised any of us on how to become rich. I rarely had two dimes in my pocket to rub together, so I began asking around for a job. It would cost more time away from college studies, but then again, I couldn't have become much worse off academically.

With all of this, it would be important to maintain the *status quo* of letting Jefferson think nothing was up and that he remained in control. At the moment he least expected, when everything was just right, I'd pull back hard on the reins he held over me and take him by surprise.

I felt a little smug about my change in attitude. Somehow, I'd regain control. Dr. J would respect me even more because of it. With this, I also decided to purchase a pipe, and elected to smoke an apple tobacco; one with an unusually strong fragrance. Thinking men were the type who smoked pipes. This would become part of my fictitious persona to demonstrate I was much smarter than he'd figured. He'd be impressed and eventually would reward me for all of this. If he was actually an author, I'd give him something good for a second book with me as the main character. One day, I'd invite Oprah on my show.

I visited the local pipe shop and inquired, "Excuse me sir; can you confirm that smart guys smoke apple pipe tobacco?"

156

Axiom Eighty-Eight
Think creatively!

How would I invent an alternate identity? I didn't know any forgers at this point in my life, so I needed to have an excuse for my lack of birth documentation.

At the library, I found a book on memorable fires in upstate New York. I located a town hall and county courthouse, which both had been destroyed in a community just north of Albany, N.Y. at about the time I was born. The municipal fires would explain the loss of an original birth certificate.

When I was up that way on an outing club trip learning to skydive, I noted from the phone book that there were a great number of "Goodwins" in that area. Wasn't there a "Goodwin" who'd come over on the Mayflower? Then and there, I became "Adam Goodwin." "Adam Goodwin" had a nice ring to it. People would trust a guy named "Adam Goodwin." A sense of pride came over me for coming up with the idea, and now, I dreamt about how I might build Adam's fictitious background.

I had a most excellent high school teacher named 'William Warden.' He really cared for his students' growth in what was certainly a difficult job. As a committed instructor, after class, he patiently taught me how to construct a composition. If I could right now, I'd pay him a thousand dollars dividend for his investment in me. He had his work cut out, because, mind you, I was nothing close to a genius. Due to his considerate help, eventually, I could write. He taught me how to formulate arguments, support these with evidence, and then how to draw conclusions. Not that I was ever excellent at writing when Mr. Warden knew me, but as I moved ahead in college, my ability improved and was probably my only advantage in the academic realm.

I gave a great deal of thought as to how to reduplicate Dr. J's tactics for my own benefit. Adam Goodwin would take some risks and do my dirty work. Somehow, Jefferson would make the link between the fictitious character and myself and he'd undoubtedly be very impressed. Just as the persona of Pete Sommers had set me in a precarious situation, so also, Adam Goodwin would return the favor in some playful sense. I felt relieved, having come up with a workable plan. I intended to astonish Dr. J.

Axiom Eighty-Nine
Compliments open doors.

Thereafter, Adam Goodwin began writing letters to the newspaper at Delphi College. In my brief excursion on the campus, I'd gained a basic familiarity with the facilities, learned a few professors' names, and the main courses of study. It was just enough that I could sound knowledgeable as a current student. Because of my ever so brief involvement with the campus paper, I'd been registered on the mailing list and received forwarded issues of the Delphi Observer. This provided me with a weekly archive of relevant material to sort through for the topic of editorials. The character of Adam wrote as if though he was a student in one of the classes making commentary on the high quality of instruction offered at the school. Of course, nobody really knew Adam Goodwin, and some of the administrators assumed it was a pen name.

The fictitious persona spoke favorably about changes at Delphi and commented highly of certain professors and the work of specific department leaders. A few controversial administrative decisions had been made, and he spun these in a way that cast a progressive light on the advancement of its thinkers. During the semester, the university newspaper published six of these as editorials.

Moving forward with the set-up, Adam also sent copies of two of his more well-written commentaries on policy deviations at the college to the Narrows Creek town paper. Goodwin's second article received a complimentary, reflective response from the main editor. Soon, the fictitious student was on his way to becoming a respected and trusted citizen with a developing history in connection with a well-known school. This was working great!

Very quickly, my alias gained notoriety as a broadminded thinker on the campus, and I wrote a letter requesting a meeting with the dean of the business department. I'd mentioned him prominently three times and had done my best to make a brilliant guy shine brightly in his administrative capacities. I needed a powerful ally at Delphi who could be used as a reference.

When he heard my name over the phone, I could tell that he was beaming with delight.

"Hello, Adam, how pleasant it is to have the opportunity to speak with you!"

I explained that I was interested in pursuing a master's degree and hoped to find a successful professor with whom to discuss strategies for business students to market themselves. Because of his familiarity with the complimentary editorials, he was eager to work me into his schedule.

About a week later, I called to verify our date, and he asked if I minded him making a few changes. The president of

Delphi University wanted to sit in on our interview, so he'd decided to open it up to the student body. He figured that there were many folks who would be interested in searching out a good path to a master's degree.

"We're going to use the questions you sent me and do this as a Q & A mini-symposium. You and I will sit together on the stage with microphones. Some of my students, other faculty members, and a few administrators will attend."

I almost fell over and hung myself on the payphone cord! I stammered, "Yes, sure, certainly, that would be outstanding."

We set up the date in two weeks on a Saturday morning. I arrived early on a Trailways Bus, with a fresh haircut, looking sharp, making my suit and tie look handsome. Several of the department head's students, who undoubtedly found themselves in academic need, were setting up tables and chairs. They had arranged bagels, cream cheese, juice, coffee, and some pastries for the event.

Everyone assumed that I must have been a local student situated on campus. I only had to ask a few prepared questions during the event and the professor would respond.

Axiom Ninety
Be careful not to get blinded by the light.

Better and beyond my most farfetched imagination, a local reporter showed up from the city paper. While I was shaking hands with both the president of the college and the department chair, I heard a "poof" and my eyes were momentarily blinded by a flash.

The camera guy remarked, "Great shot!"

A reporter from the local paper further helped my alias by including a few details about where I'd grown up and why I'd chosen this college. He wanted to know more about my plans in life and what sort of research degree I intended to pursue.

Yippee-Yye-Yeah!

Two days later, on the front page of the Monday Morning Edition of the Narrows Creek Times, a nice-looking shot of Adam Goodwin appeared, grinning ear to ear. They gave a mini-bio and a brief history of where he was born in upstate N.Y. and was later raised in New England. His father was an east coast banker who some years earlier had been a lawyer in a local law firm.

The article reported, "Adam has been articulate in commenting on newsworthy events concerning Delphi College." Further on, it continued, "The outspoken student captured the attention of instructors and administrators with reflective editorials, regarding changes recently instituted at the school."

Adam Goodwin was now not only somebody with a history, he felt as if he was about to embrace a bright future. Little did I realize that such firm establishment of an alias would very shortly result in my foreign imprisonment.

Axiom Ninety-One
Triage is a transferable skill.
When you're overwhelmed use triage.

What the heck is triage? I learned about the concept as I completed my Emergency Medical Technician training at New Paltz. EMTs exercise triage when they arrive at the scene of an accident with multiple injuries. Essentially, it's a matter of prioritizing who can be treated most effectively and efficiently.

My dire academic circumstances demanded this kind of examination. First, there was the problem with my grades. I was failing and just had to resolve to try to do my homework and study for an hour each day for my classes. I decided it was best for the remainder of the semester, not to commit to any more escapes. Mom had threatened to string me up by my ying-yang if things didn't improve. Whatever she meant by that, it sounded terribly painful.

Beyond this, I decided to allow Jacob to think he was getting under my skin. It would make him feel good to know his annoyances were having their intended results. A strategy of sucking up to him, pretending that I needed his approval, would also alleviate a measure of pressure. He'd feel important, and stroking his ego would keep him preoccupied. It was a nearly effortless way to manage his antics and perhaps a means of discovering more about the man called "Elias Jefferson," a.k.a. "Pete Sommers."

I realized the difficulty that a full investigation was going to be time-consuming and costly. I had several hundred dollars saved, but I knew my plans in figuring this guy out would require more. I began selling a few items to raise additional cash and took a job as a line worker at the Rat.

Dad was now sending me about $80 per month. Although I felt as if I needed every penny that I could scrounge, there was something sacred about his check. Whenever it showed up, I went straight to the post office and converted it to an anonymous money order and sent it off to Pastor James.

He and his wife invited us to diner on several occasions. As I poked around their house, I discovered that their cupboards and refrigerator were almost always empty. There was never enough on the table for seconds, and Mom's watchful eyes coached us on what size portions we were allowed to put on our plates.

Axiom Ninety-Two
Don't pretend to know everything.
Appearing dumb or limited in aptitude
can work to your advantage.

Dr. Adler and I had enjoyed steak, lobster, shrimp, and even frog legs. On our last meeting at the tennis club, I unveiled my supposed reduplication of what I'd originally sent off to Shilling Oil. He was thrilled at last to get his hands on the prize.

I explained, "What I really wish I had was someone as smart as you to help me dig through the maps and to evaluate the strata. I'm struggling to get this all put back together in exactly the same way that I had it the first time. I think I'm missing some important stuff, but I'm so unfamiliar with the resources that I'm lost. A guy with your expertise could probably complete this in no time at all."

In his inebriated state of mind, my professor really liked the suggestion.

I felt as if I'd gotten my proverbial pound of flesh, for Adler's manipulation of my servitude for grades at the start of the semester. The ax I had to grind had been fully ground, my vengeance was complete, and my fattened belly was good evidence. I felt a few pangs of guilt over the many lavish meals I'd extorted as I bit into another spoonful of what would be the last experience of the delicious chocolate mousse. Nevertheless, I was relieved to turn the project over to my professor and hoped all of this wouldn't come back to haunt me.

I was reminded of my agreement with the Almighty and finally sent $25 to the Bible correspondence course advertised on the radio. It was important to live up to my word and keep my end of the deal.

Axiom Ninety-Three
Money doesn't grow on trees.
Work hard. Work smart. Invest wisely.

So, along the way, I ended up getting to know Dallas Redding, owner of the tennis country club, through my friend who worked in the kitchen. The older gentleman began to recognize me when I came in for my regular weekend dining with Dr. Adler. He was building a banquet hall off the back of the building and needed someone to insulate and paint it. He paid better than the Rat, although I kept both jobs.

Axiom Ninety-Four
Be kind.
Do unto others as you would have others do unto you.

I set up the meeting in the library that I'd proposed to my professor a week earlier. I showed him the maps case and even surprised him with some geological assets he wasn't aware of in the collection. Then, I had another handmade map with tracing paper that worked as an overlay. On it were lists of the limestone strata (each layer had a certain name) and the known fossils found in those deposits. I told him that this is where I began then added some mumbo-jumbo about the importance of also identifying hilly terrain that might predict the existence of oil. He seemed to buy it as good starting ground for research and thanked me. I excused myself and he took over the project.

Not surprisingly, he turned it into legitimate research. He was now a happy brainiac and I was free, at least for the moment, to devote more energy to figuring out Jefferson.

Axiom Ninety-Five
The less that's known about you the more difficult you are to leverage.

Leverage is possible because of what you know about people. Pete Sommers had so much on me he had the potential for insurmountable control. He appeared to be a genuine friend and a beneficiary, but I wondered what his endgame really looked like. He wasn't saying.

I needed to know more about Sommers or Jefferson or whoever he really was. He called me one day to talk about an assignment. I asked if he might be able to meet me in 30 minutes behind my building at LeFevre Hall out back by the dumpster. When we got off the phone, I thought for a minute and asked my roommate for a favor for which I was willing to pay $5 in cash.

Now, these days $5 is nothing at all. At that time, though, it was quite a lot of money for such a simple job. I wanted my roommate to get Pete's license plate and any other information such as the VIN number from the windshield or anything else he could find on the car.

Brad was curious what this was all about. I offered to up the ante to the unspeakable amount of $10 if he agreed not to ask questions. I told him that I had a friend coming to see me and that we were going to run over to the Rat to grab a bite. We would be back in just a few minutes, so he might have as little as ten minutes alone by the vehicle. I warned him that he wasn't allowed to touch the car, and he couldn't be recognized snooping around. Pete and I would cut through the building toward the cafeteria, and then he'd know the coast was clear. He kind of liked the intrigue of the challenge, but said, he did it mostly because he wanted the $10.

When Pete arrived, it was a little after dinner time. He parked at the curb, got out, looked me over head to toe, and commented, "Are you putting on some weight, Levi?"

"Maybe," I replied, "but, I was just thinking about dinner." One thing I knew about Pete Sommers that I could leverage was his beneficent attitude. I rubbed my stomach theatrically and asked, "Did you eat yet?"

He replied, "No, is there anything close by?"

I knew that he knew better.

He was happy to oblige and we cut through the building. What I ended up with was far more valuable than the $10 it cost me, not to mention that I received $7 worth of food.

Axiom Ninety-Six
You get what you pay for.

"So how are things going with paleontology?"

As I responded to the question, I took out my pipe and packed it with tobacco.

I accentuated his alias in an official sounding tone, "Well 'Mr. Sommers,' I thought you'd never ask. It does seem as if I may pass the class with a grade slightly above a 'C,' thanks to your kind assistance. Actually, I want you to know that I was already moving up fast from a strong 'D+' average before you got in my way!"

He chuckled.

I lit up and smoke wafted through the air.

"Bravo, Levi!"

Dr. J offered a high-five. He caught the fragrance and said, "Apple? Very nice! I had no idea you smoked."

I brushed off his comment, "Yeah, kind of a closet smoker until recently."

I blew a little puff into the air off to the side of us and thought I might puke. No matter what it smelled like, it tasted like crap.

Even so, I kept a straight face and continued, "You know, Mom and Dad didn't really dig this when I was at home." I raised my eyebrows and suspiciously glanced to the left and right as if they might be watching. Then, I went on, "Adler thinks we're on to something, although he's gone solo on the research. You might call it a 'maps for grades deal.'"

He smirked and reached over and patted my shoulder. "Well done!"

It was roughly a year later when my professor received significant acclaim at the annual meeting of the National Geologic Examiners for his presentation and publication of a paper entitled, "Evidential Trilobites in North Sloping Strata Indicate Abundant Oil Reserves." All those dinners I'd eaten at his expense were thanks enough for me. The professor eventually retired from teaching and went on to become the director of research for a petroleum conglomerate. He wound up with a remarkable amount of money and fame. The story of his independent research and discoveries eventually appeared in Continental Geographic Magazine. He'd never know just how proud I was of him!

As for my own investment with my roommate, I got mixed results. The license plate was easy and there was a rental car sticker on the rear left side of the trunk. The VIN number, however, was covered up by several documents. I wasn't exactly sure how I'd be able to use that anyway, but I understood that the acquisition of information is nearly always synonymous with gaining power.

What intrigued me were three letters on the corner of one of the sheets of stationery he saw on the dashboard. They were initials in an embossed logo pressed through a folded page that read "IPM." Brad could tell further that it was a letter signed in cursive. He said that the imprint from the pen mark, viewed through the back of the paper, was something like "Back-Floss" or "Back-Crass." He was certain that the final letters of the last name were both "s." Otherwise, the vehicle looked clean.

I began doing research, and as it turned out, the car had been rented in Paramus, New Jersey. That led me to another search. At first, I guessed incorrectly that IPM was a corporation located nearby. Eventually, however, I found my way back to those large green business abstracts in the library and discovered what I suspected was the match. The "International Pen Manufacturing Corporation," was more than coincidentally also located in the same N.J. city.

So, now, I had a reasonable guess who Pete Sommers worked for, but it provided no logical motive as to why he was so interested in me or any of the other students on our campus.

My hunch moved in the direction that he was some sort of recruiter. I'd almost reached the conclusion that none of this could've had anything to do with a supposed book on problem-solving. What might a pen manufacturer have to do with all this silly prankish intrigue?

I wondered if IPM was connected with the individuals who were after me in the chases or if those folks were only associates of Dr. J.

Axiom Ninety-Seven
Operate within your budget.

I'd contacted a private investigator in Paramus N.J. to do some snooping around. He was a terse guy who demanded $500 down. He expected $500 more when he felt he'd gathered a grand's worth of details. OUCH! I could tell by the tone of his voice and his obnoxious attitude that explaining I was a poor college student wasn't going to elicit much pity.

I took a chance though and asked, "Do you ever work to gather $125 worth of information?"

It's tough when you're a college guy on a student budget and you're also trying to be a spy.

He replied sarcastically in a way I could tell he thought was funny, "Sure mister. Tell me what I can look up in the phone book for you!" He laughed hysterically at his smart aleck response; thoroughly enjoying himself. "Whose number are you looking for? Better yet, mister, I'm running a special today; two for the price of one." He went on cackling at his rude remarks, mocking my poverty.

Even though the investigator didn't know when to shut up, I figured that I could still use him, despite my lack of finances.

"Okay, $500 down it is! I'll pay you cash and give you the first part Monday morning. Meet me at the International Pen Manufacturing office at 3795 Orchard Grove Ave., at 7:00. My name is Adam Goodwin and I'll be heading into work there. I'll give you the rest of the details of the job with the money. Does that work for you?"

"Sure mister. I'm glad we can work a deal. I'm talented and I'll figure out whatever you need."

I closed our conversation by describing myself. "You'll recognize me by my gray hair. I'm about 50 years old and I'll be heading for the main entrance wearing a suit and tie."

I'd never seen Dr. Jefferson without a suit and tie, so it was a good bet that the plan was going to work.

I got on the Trailways bus very early, Monday morning, at about 1:00 a.m. and connected in New York City for Paramus. It turned out to be a cold, rainy, miserable day.

Axiom Ninety-Eight
Dress for success. Be versatile in appearance.

The bad weather ended up working to my advantage because it gave me a reason to wear a raincoat with a hood. Because I didn't want to be recognized, I brought several more outfits in a duffel bag.

Mind you, this took place back in the days before these cameras were mounted outside everywhere, recording everyone and tracking their movements. Big Brother, the proverbial governmental entity from George Orwell's novel Nineteen Eighty-Four, was not yet alive as he is today, looking over everybody's shoulder constantly monitoring our lives.

By the way, did you know that the microphone on your cell phone is never turned off and that your camera can be turned on remotely? Spies have it so much easier today! You innocently download a free game, a weather app, or almost any kind of software, and its creator can track your movements, monitor your email, read your texts, send email from your accounts, listen in on your conversations, look at your photos, examine the documents on your device, remotely access your bank account, and even use all of the cameras simultaneously to record videos. If Orwell could only have imagined the era of the smartphone!

When I arrived, I loitered briefly around the parking lot and managed to gather all the license plate numbers. I photographed the cars with my stealth Kodak Instamatic 110 and got shots of everyone entering and exiting the building. I'd stick around for a while as one person and then come back dressed entirely differently. At one point, I put on a wig and looked like a hobbling old lady with a cane who was innocently waiting for the bus. I blended in with the heavy foot traffic. At precisely 7:55 a.m., Dr. Jefferson arrived with his umbrella and briefcase. Two others showed up at the door within minutes. I guessed that these three worked together as a team. A larger crew arrived around 10:00 a.m.

A man driving a Ford Mustang had been sitting in the parking lot, and I guessed that he must have been the private investigator. He got out and intercepted Jefferson on the steps. The two men exchanged greetings, shook hands, and it became obvious that there was some confusion between them. I was fairly certain that I made out hearing Dr. J's statements, "No, I'm sorry, you have the wrong guy. There's nobody named 'Adam Goodwin' who works in our building."

It was difficult to hear the investigator's response because of his heavy accent and the resounding spatter of the rain. He waited around for another hour and finally drove off. He'd gotten the job done perfectly at a more reasonable budget that I could afford. Thereafter, the name and peculiarity of a supposed Adam Goodwin employee would be indelibly etched in Dr. J's mind.

I'd never considered that I might someday work for a pen manufacturer. Despite this, I looked up at the top floor corner office window with the view of the park across the street and thought, "If Jefferson turns out to be a head hunter looking for students to work in the pen industry, I'll see if I can get that office with the nice view. He'll undoubtedly recognize how smart and deserving I am from all of this!"

Among the first three entering the building, I saw a medium to good looking thirty-year-old who I just made a wild guess might

172

be Dr. Jefferson's assistant. She looked very professional and efficient, like a nurse who was a little on the serious side. Her heels clacked on the pavement as she made her way across the parking lot. Because she was the only female who entered the building before I called them from a pay phone at about 9:00 a.m., I figured I knew who I was speaking to. The young lady introduced herself as "Sharon."

"Hello, ma'am. I hope your morning is going well."

"Why thank you Mr..."

She paused waiting for me to fill in the blank.

"Oh, it's 'Mr. Smith.' I'm interested in ordering some pens with my company name stamped on the side."

She cheerfully remarked, "I am very sorry, Mr. Smith, but we're not presently taking new pen orders. At the moment, our manufacturing facility is down. Let me give you some numbers for a few other companies serving the industry."

She provided contact information for two competitors who she assured me could help.

I pretended to write all this down, but I still wanted to keep her on the line for more information.

"I'm sorry too. This is surprising." I remained silent for a moment, hoping this would put her on the defensive.

Then, I added, "What about getting some pencils?"

She further explained something about suspending sales for a corporate reorganization, which sounded like an astutely packaged load of crap. Supposedly they were expanding into copy services and printing.

Sharon asked, "I wonder if your company might be in the market for a new mimeograph machine?"

The new pitch was a clever tactic on her part to redirect the conversation into a topic that probably wouldn't interest me, thereby providing good reason to end the call. Since, I wasn't prepared for further interrogation, I thanked her for her time and the information.

After I'd hung up, I thought, "What kind of a pen company doesn't have any pens for sale?" A few hours later, I wondered, "If IPM wasn't presently taking orders, why did she try to sell me the mimeograph machine?"

Later that afternoon, I called once more, explaining, "Hello Sharon. It's Mr. Smith again. My office manager tells me that we are, in fact, in the market for a copy machine. Can you describe a few of the mimeographs you carry and the prices?"

She was exceedingly pleasant but apologetically informed me that they wouldn't have their full line in place for another two weeks or perhaps even for another month. I'd have to call back later for further information.

Amidst all of her cheerful professionalism something seemed fishy.

I really wanted to ask, "How do you manage to keep the lights on in such a large building without making any sales? Is there anything available that I can actually purchase from you today?"

I bit my tongue.

Axiom Ninety-Nine
Pay attention to details.
Look for openings.

At 11:30 a.m., Sharon left the building and was gone for about half an hour. She came back with several bags of fast food and a tray with three drinks. Therefore, I hypothesized that she, Dr. Jefferson, and the other guy had arrived early to work together on a project of some sort. She'd gone to get lunch for the team. Other than that, there wasn't anything else remarkable about traffic in and out of the building.

At 4:30, the three early arrivals left in their cars. I jotted down the directions of their departures, not that I expected this information to be very useful. I didn't have any means of following them and they could've driven anywhere. The rest of the crew departed at 6:30. It was probably going to be a long boring evening staring at my reflection in the front door of IPM. After a while, I wondered if they might receive after-hours deliveries. My bus didn't leave until midnight, so I had lots of time to think. If I'd had more money I'd have gotten a motel room and scoped out the scene a second day.

At 8:00 p.m., a floor cleaning van showed up. I thought I'd risk meeting them and find out what they knew about IPM. I walked over, "Hey guys, are you hiring?"

A stocky man with a deep voice and a thick New Jersey accent responded, "Do you have a car and can you be to work on time every night? We work a different building every night, so you have to be pretty smart with directions and always on time."

"Sure! I'd start tonight if I could." This had the possibility of being a lucky break.

"Okay, kid. Have you ever worked a buffer before?"

"No, but I do know that the floor has to be swept before buffing, and I'm familiar with stripping and re-waxing floors. I've just never run a buffer."

I knew things were looking up when he said, "The job pays $6 per hour. You good with that?"

"Yeah, that's great."

"Okay. What's your name?"

"'Adam Goodwin,' friends call me 'Goody.'" Why did I add the second part? It sounded ridiculous. It's strange what falls off your tongue when you're nervous. I hoped I wouldn't say anything else that sounded so stupid.

He continued, "Well how about if we just call you 'Adam' for now? Help Joe there with the mops and brooms."

"Terrific! Thanks! I'm happy to be on board."

"It's your lucky day Adam; or should I say your lucky night? Dave phoned in sick yesterday and didn't show up tonight. I'm Ricardo. That's Bobby and Fred. Hey Bobby and Fred! Meet 'Adam.' He's gonna' be our new 'Dave.'"

Axiom One Hundred
Miracles happen!

I was psyched because I'd found a legal way into the building! Nevertheless, it was so freaking cold, and exhaustion began to cloud my mind making it difficult to move. As soon as I made it through the front doors, however, the adrenalin was pumping. I pushed the broom with resolve. Moving in and out of several offices, I saw the fast food wrappers and cups that I

176

supposed Sharon had brought in at lunchtime. I gathered up the trash bags from three offices containing those items and moved them out to the front door. All the guys were still down the long hall at the other end of the building, so I took a second to call Brad from the desk of someone named "Jack Strauss." It was the only way I could think of to get an inside phone number, other than that of the main line which led to the receptionist. I hoped Brad wouldn't answer because his phone machine was fancy and would keep track of the number.

"Hello," I heard at the other end.

"Brad, it's Levi. I can't explain, but you need to hang up and let me call back and let the answering machine take a message. I need to get the number where I'm phoning from. Write it down and put it somewhere so we don't lose it!"

"Okay, dude!"

After this, I kept checking trash bins to see if any others had fast food wrappers in them. There were none, so it was a good bet that the desks in those rooms belonged to Dr. Jefferson, the girl, and the other guy. The desk name plates read. "Sharon Baxter," "Joshua Pengrove," and "Jack Strauss." I was perplexed at not finding an office for "Jefferson" or "Sommers."

A loud voice interrupted my deep thoughts, "Hey, Adam, what-a-ya' think you're doing?" Ricardo came out of a room and saw that I'd stacked the bags of trash by the front door. I met him there as he asked, "What are these? We ain't garbage men here, ya' know! We're floor guys."

I could tell he was a little upset. "Oh, sorry, Ricardo. I didn't realize this wasn't part of our job. I just assumed we did all of this as part of the nighttime cleaning." I shrugged at him. "Should I go ahead and throw these in the dumpster outside anyway?"

He glanced at the collection of translucent trash can liners and pushed one off another with his foot to get a better look at the contents.

"Sure kid. Get rid of them, then finish the backside hallway."

"Yes, sir."

I was outside the doorway and disappeared behind the dumpster, where I'd hidden my duffel bag. I quickly sorted out everything that wasn't lunch leftovers and packed up all the rest of the papers for the trip home. Then, I high-tailed it back down to the bus station.

Along the way, I thought, "Dang!" One of those guys had left nearly all of their fries untouched, but they were cold now. Probably that chick, watching her figure! Those would've made a nice snack. Ugh.

I mulled over not having found a desk for either, "Pete Sommers" or anyone named "Jefferson." I figured that he had to be Joshua or Jack. What was it with all these "J" names?

During the ride home, between dozing off and waking up and due to the general discomfort of sleeping while sitting up, I made the spelling connection between "Jack Strauss" and the cursive impression through the paper that Brad interpreted as "Back-Floss." Was Dr. J, a.k.a. Pete Sommers, actually named "Jack Strauss?"

As I waited for my cab in New Paltz, I became more certain that Jefferson was, indeed, actually "Jack Strauss." He'd been approached on the steps of his workplace by a stranger looking for someone named "Adam Goodwin" that morning. There was a chance that he might also hear the name again from the floor crew. Maybe in a week or so, I could start mailing some belongings to IPM, care of Jack Strauss, that belonged to Adam Goodwin. I'd start with a nice desk name label matching theirs. That would be funny. Then, after that, when he came to visit again, I could eventually use his real name and ask, "So 'Jack,' do you have my office set up yet?"

Axiom One Hundred One
Substantiate your alias with props.

I was on the phone at 8:00 a.m. the next morning sniffling and sneezing. I'd obviously contracted an upper respiratory bug in Paramus. After finding the cold medicine I followed up on my idea to order a few items for my new office at IPM.

"Hello, Ma'am. My name is 'Adam Goodwin,' and I need to order a desk nameplate. I have about thirty dollars to spend."

"I'll be glad to assist you with your order, sir. Have you seen something in our catalog that you find appealing or would you like me to make some suggestions?"

"Well, to be honest, I found your name in the 'World Abstract of Commerce and Trade.' I haven't seen any samples, but I have something in mind."

She sounded so kind and endearing, "Go ahead and describe it, sir, and I'll tell you what we have."

"I'd like something with a black background and gold raised letters. I've seen them before mounted on a dark colored block of wood."

"That sounds like our C.E.O. series. How about if I mail you a brochure."

"That won't be necessary. I'd like to go ahead and order it now, if possible?"

Doris, from "Office Tradeworks Unlimited ltd.," explained their phone sales and return policy, which didn't allow for any returns under any circumstances. She inquired, "What kind of credit card will you be using today?" I hid my embarrassment over not having plastic. We settled on her processing payment by check, which took as little as 2 days, after it arrived by mail. The first order waited for release until they'd received the funds from the bank. Subsequent orders could then be placed with immediate shipment on good faith for established customers.

The problem was that she was about to leave for a two-week vacation. If she didn't receive payment the next day, I'd have to wait several weeks. There went another $20 at the post office for next day service!

A day after I figured that the first order had been mailed, I placed a second for a monogrammed pen and ruler set.

IPM would be receiving two shipments of desktop supplies that had cost me dearly and which would undoubtedly raise questions.

Having anticipated refusal of the delivery, I explained, "Doris, I have a big favor to ask that I also need you to keep in confidence."

"Oh?" she replied.

"You see, The International Pen Manufacturing Company is about to go through a management change. There is a small chance that they'll receive the orders before everyone at the office is aware of my arrival."

She responded inquisitively, "Really?"

"So, I'm certain if this happens that you'll be contacted about the return of the items."

Doris quickly interjected, "And of course, I've already explained that these sales are final."

"Yes, ma'am. I promise you that I won't be returning anything. But, I need you to remain adamant about the fact that they need to keep the items for, 'a new employee who says he's coming on board soon.' Assure them that there is no mistake, but also, please don't give them my contact information."

Doris was smart. "This is beyond our normal range of services, but I have an idea, Mr. Goodwin. We're just getting set to mail out the second order today. How about if I include a note with the pen set, acknowledging the unusual nature of the shipment for an employee who is to be soon in his arriving? I will also affirm that this isn't a mistake and that we've double checked everything to assure IPM that they should hold on to the items."

"That sounds terrific!" Sometimes I had a way of complicating things and I was grateful for her ability to streamline the process.

Axiom One Hundred Two
When you don't cover your tracks you leave a trail.

"Hello, Mr. Pengrove, this is Ricardo Sanchez."

"Hey Ricardo, did they miss sending out your check again? You guys do such a great job around here. We would hate to lose you!"

"Thank you for asking sir, but everything is just fine with our account payment. I'm calling because I had a problem last night."

"Oh, is everything okay?"

"I think so, sir, but I wanted to let you know about it just in case."

"Did something happen here?"

"Yes, sir. I hired a new kid. He approached us at your door looking for work. My regular guy, Dave, hadn't shown up for two nights, so the kid was in the right place at the right time. I put him on the crew, and he worked fine for the first three hours. Now maybe this is just nothing to worry about, and I got to say that he didn't know our routine, so probably everything is okay. But, here is what happened. While he was sweeping, the kid also began gathering trash from the offices and put it by the front door. I told him we don't do that and went over and looked at the bags. I could see through some of the clear liners. They contained a bunch of papers and some food wrappers, so I told him to go toss it in the dumpster and to get back to work with the broom. After he took it out, he disappeared. It was weird. Then, I got to thinking that I hoped he hadn't stolen anything by hiding it in what he carried outside the building. I'm insured and bonded, so if you guys find you are missing anything, I'll get it replaced. I'm so sorry if this causes you any trouble."

Joshua heard a huge sigh of frustration over the phone.

"Well Ricardo, thank you for telling me about this. I'll let the others know and we'll have a look around. It may just be that the guy was being conscientious about work and was going the extra mile; then decided he didn't want the job after all."

"Yeah, maybe I spooked him when I raised my voice about the trash."

"Do you have his phone number and contact information?"

"No, sir. I just hired him on the spot and we began unloading the truck. I figured I'd get all his information later. I can describe just what he looks like if that helps."

"And what was his name?"

"It was 'Adam Goodwin.'"

Axiom One Hundred Three
Be careful what you throw in your trash!

I was so sick that it took another several days before I could sort through my gleanings from the IPM trash.

Pengrove's wastebasket had all these files with details on different kinds of people from all over the world. They looked like important dudes. He must have been a researcher or something. He had quite a bit in there. One paper had some hand-written notes on the side with the name "Josef." Was he the same guy I knew? I bet it was. Maybe my I.Q. test was stashed away in his office somewhere!

His trash also included a few formatted cover sheets with some rich guys' names on them that listed most of their assets, bank holdings, and personal information. These even had detailed facts about the academies those people's children attended, the times they arrived, and were dismissed. The list of facts included work schedules, doctor's names, prescribed medications, and so on. There were check boxes for who rode the bus, who walked, and who was dropped off by a car at work or at school; including the driver's names. It looked like information was being gathered as some kind of reconnaissance.

I began to get a sick feeling, as I continued rummaging through the mess. The papers had lots of names, many of them foreign in nature. There were also cities mentioned from around the world. In all of this there were facts about people who were obviously being watched, and a tremendous amount of data was being collected about their lives.

As I read, one thing became obvious to me. The reason IPM didn't have any pens to sell was that they were actually a giant worldwide spy organization. My mind was racing. Had I blown it big time with my idiotic, show-off antics? What kind of mess had I gotten myself into?

I'd used the private investigator like a pawn on the front steps of IPM to plant the name "Adam Goodwin" in the mind of Dr. Jefferson, or rather, Jack Strauss. My intention was to turn the tables on the gray-haired man and to eventually play a huge joke. I just wanted to prove to him that I was the one in control of my life. I'd ordered the desktop items to mess with him. The thought of these artifacts arriving to the bewildered staff at IPM made me feel smug when I'd come up with the idea. It wasn't enough to have some guy writing a book about me. I'd felt compelled to learn more about his plans and to turn his project into something bigger. It was part of the Martin DNA. Now, I just felt sick over the whole mess.

I had figured that eventually, I'd spring myself on Jack as "Adam Goodwin" in a way that made me look just as clever as him. Somehow, the alias would have added to my fame, or so, I thought.

Now, however, there was a serious problem. All of this was going to backfire because IPM might also hear the name of "Adam Goodwin" from the floor cleaning crew along with the story of his ever so short employment. It was pretty likely that they'd discover it was me who'd stolen this secret information.

Even the missing clear plastic trash liners would be a clue. I should have replaced those or only taken part of the contents from the cans. CRAP!

I wanted to kick myself! What an idiot! Here, I thought I was so stinking smart, but now, I became so angry that I shouted at myself, "You imbecile!" My shortsighted actions had changed everything. If they began searching for "Adam Goodwin," it wouldn't be long before they'd locate his photo in a recent Narrows Creek Times story. How could I have been such a numbskull? The habitual role of trying to outsmart everyone had boomeranged back at me with what might prove to be lethal force. In the least, it was going to get me into a great deal of trouble.

Although I'd pursued the plan to investigate every organization and extracurricular gathering on the campus, I'd been having loads of fun, and I'd become too absorbed in the antics of my own world. Had I lost sight of the goal of the larger collegiate picture? I should have kept both eyes open and stayed focused on the plan! But, no, I proved I was a Martin tried and true. This wasn't the way things were supposed to have happened.

A sweeping fear came over me with the question, "Had I screwed up my whole purpose after transferring to New Paltz?" Could I still save things? How? I had to think fast.

Axiom One Hundred Four
Assemble the puzzle and learn.

After I calmed down a little, I began pouring through the information and examining the contents I'd gathered more closely. Maybe there was another way out of this.

Sharon Baxter appeared to be some sort of doctor. She'd discarded some medical receipts, pharmaceutical advertisements, junk mail, and payment records to drug companies; some of which were copies. There were also spreadsheets quantifying names, coded symbols for medications, dosages, and reported side effects. I recognized the name "Josef" again, next to the cipher "AB112." Was this the same guy with whom I'd played chess? Under the "Side Effects" column, the comment was listed, "slight increase in heart rate—5 b.p.m., processing speed quadrupled with increase dosage of .5 mg." Was he taking a stimulant? Why?

Jack Strauss had schedules for two different tennis competitions and a pile of logistical notes on half sheets of lined writing paper. These had something to do with meetings, and they listed who, when, what, and where, along with information being gathered or actions that were being taken. There were also some financial memos. Other pieces were coded, so they didn't make any sense at all. IPM was obviously hiding city names and addresses.

"Manny – Marscony Street, 238923938 Tuesday 1:00 am, bottle break, $80 to Rivers – Laura watch – Report to Rintan Wednesday."

Another read:

"Randy – Abalone Circle, 044848584 – plant note from boss – afternoon - $0 – Lester watch – report Alex."

There were loads of these. I also found several comments concerning phone conferences with dates and mostly just first names.

"Peter – Alvin Walters – Call Thursday 2:15 pm – 3rd news alert – Peter watch – report Maxwell."

186

As I sorted through hundreds of these, I remembered that in Jack's office he had many papers stuck on the wall. My best guess was that these comprised visual calendars. The forms provided a means of tracking and project management. When each task was complete, the slip received a bold red checkmark, the information was quantified elsewhere, and the sheets were discarded.

Finally, I was able to determine that the small details were transferred to a larger biographical sheet where they were assimilated as if operatives were following a sequential plan. Such was the case on everyone they were tracking. There was also a running set of notes regarding actions that either had been taken or that were about to occur with respect to each person on whom they were spying.

One thing was certain, IPM kept its staff busy. This "Pengrove" guy was a researcher. He had all sorts of remarks scribbled on scrap paper that could be connected to, what I called, "workflow summaries." Although the pieces I had were incomplete, soon, I was able to cross reference parts of Joshua Pengrove's information to the biographical sheets from Strauss's trash. I found one on the lined half sheets of paper that read:

"Mark – confirm academy pick up Rajesh – 3:15 pm Wednesday – Mark watch – report Joshua."

Then, in Joshua's records I found a cover sheet on a man who owned a business in another country. One of his children was listed as "Rajesh." Next to his name the checkbox for school pickup was marked and then the hand-written note: "waited 29 minutes for pick up at 4:25 pm, Omar driver, black Mercedes sedan, front of Rusche Academy."

Some of these sounded frightening:

Mark – taken hostage, 934920330 P.T. – determine if alive – report Scott.

All the sudden, I found myself worrying about, "Mark," a guy I'd never met. I was somewhat relieved when I discovered another slip that appeared to be a follow-up message:

Mark alive – presently held at 23893849 P.T. – Assigned Parental names now Doris & Ben – continue watch Scott.

A chill went down my spine when I read another:

"Pete – meet Levi N.P. – Tuesday 5:15 - Shilling Oil Co. – level 2 FDT report - Pete watch – report Maxwell."

I knew, immediately, that "Pete" was short for "Pete Sommers." But, what the heck was a "level 2 FDT?" It must have been a code referencing embedded information regarding the Shilling Oil ruse that I'd been a part of with Dr. Adler. So, Pete or Jefferson or whoever he was had, indeed, been keeping track of me. Why? Then, it dawned on me. Boy, was I stupid; just plain stupid. Nobody was writing a book on problem-solving! My hopes of appearing on Oprah's show were suddenly shattered.

In all cases of these documents, someone assigned the project and then, after observing, reported back to an IPM worker. Whatever information was collected, became part of the web of a more permanent updated record. They were following a prescribed set of steps leading toward, what I guessed was an intervention in the lives of the people they were following. Each person and action were factored together as individual parts of a larger game-plan. Older notes that focused on individual completed tasks were discarded. This explained the various types of forms in my possession. I was obviously missing a summary of their goals for each of the people on whom they'd collected information and that they were targeting. Wowza!

Closing my eyes for a moment to come to grips with all of this, I listened carefully for a lesson from the formative voice of Mom, but I found myself lost in a stern silence. I pictured her staring at me with arms folded and a look that said, "Wait till your father gets home!"

I felt like an arrow that someone fired blindly deep into the heart of a wooded forest, and yet, I'd miraculously managed to hit a carefully hidden bullseye. How was my goofing off along the way going to affect the outcome? Was my screw up irreparable?

Axiom One Hundred Five
Establish yourself in a way that makes you memorable.

The talented researcher, Mr. Joshua Pengrove called to order the meeting for the executives of IPM. After graduating from the Penn State Law program *Magna Cum Laud* and working on Wall Street for five years at "Collegiate Capital Investment Holdings Inc.," the gifted investigator was finally made aware of his actual employer. In those early years in N.Y., he'd discretely provided IPM with terrific intel on multimillionaires, their holdings, transactions, trading patterns, money flow, and a plethora of financial information. He'd gathered copies of signatures, account numbers, passwords, and other intel, pertaining to the fiduciary concerns of banks and holding companies around the world. It didn't take him long to track down Adam Goodwin.

Joshua opened the discussion, "Good afternoon ladies and gentlemen. We've never had an incident quite like this before and our compromise earlier in the week is actually quite intriguing."

He shuffled a few papers around and continued, "The 'Adam Goodwin character,' and I'll explain the use of the term 'character' momentarily, has been associated with a school in Narrows Creek, N.Y. He's written a series of published editorials on the progress of academic and administrative changes taking place at Delphi College. Although he's received public accolades and some local notoriety, with further checking, I do not find any present or previous academic enrollments for the name 'Adam Goodwin.' I looked into his birth records, but the town he was born in suffered a fire and many of the registered documents at the county courthouse were destroyed. This may explain the lack of a certificate of live birth or other records referencing his parents' names and addresses. In an interview with a local reporter, he mentioned that his father was an attorney with a law firm in New England. We're considering this question."

"Where the story actually becomes interesting is that Jack Strauss has been working with a student from SUNY New Paltz. He is one of two potentials who passed all the level 1-3 tests. He eluded a canine unit and five officers in cars and on foot trailing him in the Forty Minute Chase. I know that's hard to believe, but both police reports from the SUNY campus security and the New Paltz Police Dept. are on the table for any who are interested."

"Recently, Mr. Martin was set up in a level 2 FDT. He did remarkably well with that project. It's now a wrap. He regained control and has worked his professor at the school in ways that might make an entertaining pilot for a mini-series. Levi is entering the third stage, toward limited invitation as an M.C. with the potential to come on as an intern through KCCU. He's shown promise or exceeded expectations in four out of five categories."

Axiom One Hundred Six
Work on getting good grades!

"Mr. Martin's academics are another story. He is a first semester student and has failed or underperformed in nearly every class with the exceptions of Racquet Ball, Jogging and his EMT training. Nevertheless, he proved to be tremendously clever and managed to obtain a reasonable passing grade in the geology course he was failing prior to the FDT."

Pengrove nodded to Strauss, "Lights?"

The fluorescent tubes flickered off and two photos became visible on the wall.

He returned to the exposé. "What 'Adam Goodwin' and 'Levi Martin' have in common is appearance. On the left, Adam Goodwin is pictured shaking hands with dignitaries of the university he claims to attend. On the right, you see Levi Martin in his afternoon running routine. There can be little chance that these are not the same person." Strauss interjected, "unless they are identical twins of different parents."

Pengrove continued, "However unlikely it may seem, we're convinced that somehow Martin or Goodwin was able to track Strauss' travels back to Paramus. The odds of this happening may seem next to impossible because of our procedures and the use of rental cars. But then again, what can we expect from a guy who manages to escape from a canine unit that has him cornered and trapped in a locked closet?"

A few looks of astonishment went around the room. Someone whispered, "Really?" Another replied, "If he survives to become an M.C., we need to code name him 'Houdini.'"

Joshua pointed at the table in front of himself, "Two different accounts of the chase and eventual escape are available here." Everyone was focused on the photos illuminating the wall.

"You've all heard the story of how he gained entry into the building Monday night. We have nothing new to add. It doesn't appear that he took anything, but the trash. This included some of my own research material, personal files on targets, medical records Sharon had discarded for some of the M.C.s, and project line feeds that had been assigned and completed by Jack's office. We've followed daily lockdown procedures, so nothing else important could have been stolen. Heretofore, all shredding will take place twice a day, before lunch and at closing. Based on our discussions with the floor cleaning crew, we retraced his steps through our building that night and don't find evidence that anything is missing. For the time being, we feel as if our foreign operatives are safe. Sharon, Jack and I have all done our best to recreate the items that would have been in our trash. This guy does have three info packs on targets under surveillance with partially completed summary sheets from my office. However, all the names are aliases that are coded, so we're confident these are nearly useless. Again, the documents were all assigned to first names only. Those can't lead very far. Medication names are substituted with letters and numbers. Jack's project notes might be tied to several of the target summary sheets, but they still will be of no use for real-time identification. As for our front organizations, none of their information was taken, therefore, compromise of the M.C.'s identities or those of our second or third tier employees isn't possible."

Axiom One Hundred Seven
Keep people guessing.

Jack Strauss took over momentarily, "There's one oddity to the whole thing. As I headed up the stairs Monday morning, I was stopped by a gentleman who claimed to be here to meet an employee named 'Adam Goodwin.' I explained there was nobody working at IPM by that name, and he apologized saying that there must have been some confusion. At the time, I didn't think too much of it. I figured the guy had the wrong address. Then, after Joshua informed me about Ricardo Sanchez' call, I began to wonder if something was being set up. Why a stranger would be looking for Levi Martin here and using an alias doesn't make sense. If Levi had somehow tracked me here and planned to sneak in, why would he use an alias; or for that matter, use it to meet someone on our doorstep? The two identities and the way they were used adds a great deal of mystery to the situation."

"Another oddity occurred three days ago and then yesterday. First, we received a desk nameplate and then a monogrammed pen set from 'Office Tradeworks Unlimited, Ltd.'"

He placed these on the table and everyone saw the lavish display that read "Adam Goodwin," on the top and then "IPM Management" on the byline.

"It appears as if he wanted us to expect the arrival of his alias. We're perplexed at this, however, because if Levi Martin discovered IPM, we can't reason why the kid would go to such lengths to invent an alternate identity. The pen set included an equally perplexing letter."

Dear Sir or Madame at IPM Corporation,

   We've been asked to ship these items to your office in light of the soon arrival of a new employee. We've double checked the information on the order and there is no mistake. Please hold these items for the arrival of Mr. Adam Goodwin.

Thank you,

Doris Lang

Office Tradeworks Unlimited, Ltd.

   "I called Doris, but she's out for a two-week vacation."

   A balding man at the end of the table asked, "Do we think he's a mole?"

   "Good question!" responded Joshua. "The one liability we incur from the missing documents is that they can be pieced together to show what kind of an organization IPM actually is. Just the same, nothing can be proven by any of it. If he's just some punk, then he's probably scared right about now. If he's a mole, then he knows with certainty what IPM is up to. At the moment, we don't feel as if we're in imminent danger, because he doesn't have any specific facts."

   The balding man spoke, "Our next step then?"

   "The investigation is almost complete. His fingerprints didn't show up on the radar. That lowers the odds that he could be working for a present or former target."

   Jack interjected, "That is unless he was subcontracted."

   Joshua nodded in agreement and continued, "We're open to suggestions, but our responses might range from either completely ignoring the invasion and waiting for a confession or going to the extreme of initiating a level 5 TFT. Due to the suspect's use of an alias and our unanswered questions, we're leaning toward the latter."

Looks of surprise moved like a wave over the listener's countenances. "TFT" stood for "Transported Forced Test."

The bald man asked, "Wouldn't that be considered kidnapping if it was done against his will? And why are you saying 'initiate?'"

Joshua acknowledged his superior's concerns with a stern nod. "Don's team is working on a collection of responses, and he's scheduled to make a presentation tomorrow morning. Sharon has already begun the cover for the TFT. As for the well-chosen term 'initiate,' the fact of the matter is that our target may not be on a round trip back to the states."

The bald man reflected, "I guess if we lost him in the field overseas, it would be difficult for anyone to impose litigation in Paramus upon an entity that doesn't actually exist."

Joshua agreed, "Precisely. Nobody on another continent is going to be able to link him to us."

His superior continued, "Or, we could end the whole matter quietly by allowing the kid to become one of those college students who run down to N.Y. City for the weekend and then disappears. We'd stow his body in the basement walk-in freezer and save the corpse for a future project."

Old Baldy glanced around studying the faces of his staff. He interrupted their stupefied silence saying, "However, there may be other ways that we can use him and we'll explore every option that Pengrove and the others have to offer."

He turned on his heel and held up a hand, signifying that he wasn't yet finished. "I've always regretted the possibility of saying this, but we may have to fall back."

The others stared in silence comprehending the vast implications of his last statement. "Falling back" meant the incalculable cost of dismantling the entire first tier of the IPM Corporation.

"Depending upon the degree to which we've been compromised, it may be time. Look, whatever you come up with, the solution should help us sort out the motives of this young man. Is he somehow on our side? Can we possibly trust him? Or, do we venture to lose him overseas? He could appear to be another one of those unpredictable college guys who ran off to sow his wild oats and then disappeared forever. Some kids are just unlucky that way."

Everyone understood the ominous nature of the last statement and reference to the "walk-in freezer." It was something they didn't like to think about and some of them wished they'd never been made aware of the twenty frozen corpses in the basement. The gathering stared back at the bald man in silence.

Baldy concluded, "Our next step, whether it appears friendly or hostile, needs to be a move toward cleaning this up and making it go away. You guys are the pros. Give it some thought, and let me know our best course of action."

Axiom One Hundred Eight
Be careful what you ask for.

After three nights of an exhausting lack of sleep, due to bronchitis I contracted on my trip to Paramus, I began to get really, really scared. Whatever IPM was into was big. I considered myself lucky for having gotten away with all this. What terrific fortune to have also been hired on to Ricardo's crew! Now, however, there was no backing out. No way. I couldn't just fold the hand and walk. They knew I knew too much and weren't going to let me ride off in the sunset and disappear.

Considering my circumstances, the original euphoria of the Paramus adventure faded quickly. If only I could suddenly become "John Smith" and find a place to hide! What if I promised the Almighty that I'd be extremely good for the rest of my life and maybe even reconsidered the idea to become a missionary in Africa? Pastor James used to say, "The Lord is most attentive to personal sacrifice. He notices when we devote our lives to his service." I began to ponder that my lifespan might be near its end. I hate to admit, but I wallowed in unproductive misery for almost a day. I began lamenting the loss of the imaginary world of Shilling Oil and my country club meals at Dr. Adler's expense.

I realized that I had to snap out of my bad case of the "If-onlys." There were no "ifs," "ands," or "buts" about it! It was up to me to figure out my next step, and I needed to be proactive. Where was I going from here? This was far worse than the predicament I'd found myself in with my geology professor. I realized that I'd jumped out of the frying pan into the fire and wondered about Pete Sommers' a.k.a. Elias Jefferson's a.k.a. Jack Strauss' next move. What would I do if I were him? After

197

some thought, I concluded that he'd want to get me back down to Paramus. Could I continue my Adam Goodwin ruse and push the envelope in light of my new revelations about IPM? If I went back on my own to revisit their office, it would be the last thing they'd expect. Somehow, I could try to turn this into a big joke.

Axiom One Hundred Nine
Pretense about giving away money is a key to obtaining personal information.

It only took a couple phone calls before I figured out that "Sharon Baxter" was really "Sharon Baxter." I knew her address and even learned the high school and colleges where she graduated. She'd dated the football captain, "David Jeffreys," but they broke up just before she'd moved out of her parents' home. She was now almost a doctor. It's amazing how helpful a guidance counselor can be, when he thinks you're trying to give away scholarship money.

I'd learned something simple and valuable from the private investigator who was briefly working for me. The phone book is a great source of information. Joshua Pengrove's address showed that he was in a duplex living next to "Alfred and Elizabeth Pengrove." I figured that those must be his parents. The rest of his background remained a mystery. The most useful find on Jack Strauss was that he belonged to a local tennis club. I was able to find out the date and time of his next match.

Axiom One Hundred Ten
IPM kept good records. Keep good records.

Doing humorous sorts of things had always provided a relief valve to escape from the pressures of life. While saturating my gullet with chicken noodle soup and ramen to nurse my illness, I came up with the first part of my next step with IPM.

I contrived a plan to imitate the kinds of reconnaissance documents I brought back from the trash to make it appear as if Joshua Pengrove and Jack Strauss were investigating Sharon Baxter. I took everything I knew about her that was real and made a facsimile of one of the three biographical summary forms I'd found. Then, I filled in the rest and added information making it look as if she'd dated a long list of guys on sports teams in high school up to David Jeffreys. Afterward, I included several well-known college players, including comments summarizing the conclusion that Baxter was a sports star stalker. The walls of her home were supposedly covered with posters of single athletes from the NBA and NFL.

As a woman scorned, she'd apparently suffered a long series of heartbreaks, mostly with basketball stars and football players. Nevertheless, she'd recently discovered her mailman played minor league baseball and was working to develop a romance with him. The notes read he was reciprocating and that she had strong hopes about this present beau.

There was a big stack of the forms I made like those from Jack's office that read:

Baxter P. – love relationships – age 17 to present – Jacob – report Pengrove.

Baxter P. – list connections to NFL stars – age 24 to present – Joshua watch – report Jack.

Baxter P. – verification of recent rendezvous with letter carrier - 1:00-300 Wednesday – Jack watch – report to Josh – man left with lipstick on collar.

Then, on the summary report that looked like Pengrove's, but with a few formatting improvements, I included a long list of love flings she'd been in and out of for the last half dozen years.

I became so amused with the project that I sat at my desk and laughed for an hour or so. Her most recent love had dropped her upon discovering that she couldn't sing. Before long, Sharon Baxter's dating life appeared to be a comedic event with a list of guys larger than Imelda Marcos' collection of high heels. I had a plan!

Axiom One Hundred Eleven
When it's too good to be true, then it's too good to be true.

The weekend came and I was regaining strength. You get lots of junk mail as a student, but today, I had received something useful. It was an offer for certain students to spend 2 weeks of winter break in Florida doing work-study in a marine geology program. Geological Engineering majors could qualify for a full scholarship plus a $300 stipend. If invited to stay longer, participants would be further compensated. It could lead to immediate short or long-term employment. If the work study necessitated a leave of absence from school, students could also apply for additional college credits; so long as the field work was aligned with one's major. It sounded great!

I called Mom. She and Dad agreed, considering my poor grades, this might be a good opportunity.

"If you go, we will miss you, son."

I phoned the 800 number and a receptionist took down my information. She said she just had to confirm my enrollment at SUNY, New Paltz and put me on hold. I realized that this would also allow me to disappear from IPM for a while. Maybe I wouldn't even come back!

I was momentarily relieved that I hadn't taken the plunge and hastily offered myself to the Almighty as a missionary to Africa. It wouldn't be the first time that my choice disappointed Pastor James.

About three minutes later, that seemed like an eternity, she was back on the line and confirmed that I'd been accepted.

"Well, Levi, it looks as if you've filled our last opening." She asked, "Do you think you'll enjoy some free time on the warm sunny beaches?"

Hello! Need she have asked? The plane tickets arrived three days later for a small charter flight non-stop to Orlando!

My roommates couldn't believe it. "You are so stinking lucky! Hey, and you better bring us back T-shirts!" They began rattling off their sizes.

Axiom One Hundred Twelve
Remain sly with what you know.

Dr. J stopped by several days later. He wanted to present me with a challenging opportunity on the second day of winter break. I told him the exciting news about Florida. He seemed disappointed but was also glad for me.

He joked, "What? With your vast improvement in geology grades, you probably deserve this!"

It was the first time I'd ever declined an offer from Dr. J, alias Pete.

"Thanks for that whole huge game you played on my professor. Hey, by the way, what's up with having two different names?"

"I think I'm like you Levi. I thought it would be challenging to set you up and was curious what you would do with it. That required an alias. You impressed me, and it sounds as if you've gained some respect from Dr. Adler."

He didn't really answer my question. His response was just flattery and misdirection.

"Will there be any more parties coming up?"

"No, not until the next semester begins. I try to host gatherings for new students to meet others and to have some good old-fashioned, clean fun. I'm always on the lookout for students who might assist me with my writing research." He paused for a moment then added, "When does your work-study end? Maybe you would be willing to M.C. one of the next gatherings?"

It was a compliment to receive the offer, but I changed the subject, asking, "And what about your book?"

"Well, as for the title, it's going to be called, 'Innovative Solutions.' Some of your accomplishments will make good stories. After the break, let's have lunch and discuss the project."

During the conversation, there was a great difficulty in separating the imaginary identity of "Elias Jefferson" from my new revelations about "Jack Strauss." I wasn't sure if he knew about my "Adam Goodwin" alias yet or not. If he was aware, he didn't let on about it.

Carrying on this conversation of pretense, in light of knowing his real identity, made me dizzy. I was relieved when he finally left.

Axiom One Hundred Thirteen
Don't forget to pray.

The balding man stopped by Joshua Pengrove's office and peeked in for a moment, "Have you prepared Adam Goodwin's passport yet?"

"It's here. It's even already stamped for trips he made to Germany and France last year. He arrived in Berlin, left from Frankfurt and spent a week in Paris."

"Where's the TFT going to take place?"

"We're still deciding. It depends on our interview once we have him down here. His parents and roommates think he's going to Florida for a work-study program. We've already prepared a few postcards from the sunny beaches in his handwriting."

"Good, I think we'll get answers to some questions when he finds himself sitting on some distant edge of no-mans-land."

Axiom One Hundred Fourteen
If you feel like something is up,
just figure that something really is up.

I got to thinking about my last meeting with Dr. J. and realized that our discussion had a different tone than any of the others. It was subtle, but it almost was too normal; lacking the same quality of animation I was used to with him.

What was Strauss thinking? Had Ricardo told anyone at IPM about 'Adam Goodwin?' I decided he knew and figured that this explained my odd feeling about his visit. It was time to revisit Paramus.

Axiom One Hundred Fifteen
When the going gets tough,
the tough stay with the mission.

The trip to IPM was long but not nearly as cold as the last time. Mom always used to warn me when I went out without a coat, "You're going to freeze your diddly-whopper off out there!" Well, I had worn my long-johns this time and regrettably was sweating something else off for the whole bus ride.

I'd planned carefully to get all of this done, only hours before I'd depart from LaGuardia Airport to Orlando. I'd heard rumors that traffic patterns in and around the facility were a mixed up, jumbled mess. Getting to one's flight on time could be a problem for late arrivals. I hoped I'd be able to find my way around and that the plane would leave on time just in case I ended up with a tail from Paramus. The Trailways bus system had become my new bunk bed, and I planned to catch some shut-eye along the way.

I'd timed everything to swing by Sharon Baxter's house with an envelope full of investigation slips, several hours before she'd leave for work. These made it appear as if she'd been the subject of a lengthy IPM investigation. I planned to pin these to her windshield with a wiper blade.

Next, I'd head over to the tennis club locker room and arrive when Strauss began his match. I was fully armed with a lighter and an incendiary device comprised mostly of apple pipe tobacco to set off while he was out on the court. I had some carefully prepared facsimiles of the investigation sheets to slip into his locker. I'd leave a pair of racquetball goggles somewhere nearby as my unmistakable signature.

My bag also included a replica of one of the formatted biographical sheets I'd retrieved from Joshua Pengrove's trash. It was nicely completed with Sharon Baxter's personal information. These were wrapped in a package with an invitation to dinner at Dino's Pizza that was just down the street. By the time they went there to meet me, I'd already be on my flight to Florida.

So far as keeping up appearances was concerned, I'd fabricated a believable courier uniform from pieces obtained at "Sal's Boutique" in New Paltz – That's how we referred to the "Salvation Army Thrift Store."

I left a boxed gift at Dino's with the owner for "Jack, Sharon, and Joshua." It was a journal I entitled "Innovative Solutions," explaining start to finish how I had discovered IPM. They'd have a couple of weeks to think it all over and to digest the story. It would be a while before they caught up with me back in New Paltz. Meanwhile, I'd also be in a happier part of the world. I figured this would provide a surprising and cheerful end to the problem I'd created.

The last step of my plan, before heading back to N.Y. City with Trailways was to make one last visit to IPM. Jack would still be at the tennis club, so I was safe from anyone at IPM recognizing me. I intended to enter through the front door with a delivery for Mr. Joshua Pengrove. I was thinking this was going to be so stinking funny! What was I thinking? Was I even thinking at all? Could I pronounce all three syllables of "fron-tal-lobe?" Was I able to define "idiot?"

Axiom One Hundred Sixteen
People don't always see things the way you intended.

My deliveries to Sharon and Dino's went great that morning. At the tennis club, the pipe tobacco smoker worked like a charm, saturating the air of the locker room with its sweet aroma. Jack finished his match, retired to the locker room, and saw the racquet ball goggles sitting on the bench where he usually changed. Then he recognized the strong, apple fragrance. With all of this, he mumbled questioningly to himself, "Levi?" When he reached inside his locker for his change of clothes, he discovered a stack of investigation sheets that I had slid through the vertical vent slots in the metal door. Then a note fell from the rest of the papers which read:

"One point at a time, that's a reliable strategy! Cheers!"

I left no doubt in his mind about the fact that Levi Martin was somehow controlling the engagement.

When I arrived at IPM, I started out okay putting on a theatrical show with my delivery. I stood at the receptionist's kiosk and read the nameplate, "Aubrey Edmonds."

I greeted her, "Hello, Ms. Edmonds. I have a package for a 'Mr. Pengrove.'"

I shuffled through a few papers on a clipboard and looked all serious as if I were organizing some documentation.

She replied, "Sure, you can take that to his office."

As I walked down the hall, I realized I'd made a miscalculation. How would a new delivery guy know the way around a building he'd never been in before?

Joshua was just hanging up the phone, saying, "Great Jack! I'll keep my eyes open. Thanks."

The researcher looked up at me and smiled.

Pengrove greeted me warmly and shook my hand, "I'm so glad to meet you in person Mr. Goodwin." He gripped my hand more tightly without letting go and continued, "You and I have lots to talk about."

Axiom One Hundred Seventeen
Have an emergency escape plan.

I hadn't formulated an endgame that included a plan "B." My goal was merely to get in and get out. I had to impress these guys. If they were recruiting me, I needed to prove myself in order to secure that corner office on the top floor overlooking the park. I wanted them to read the fortuitous word on my forehead "overachiever." As things wound up though, I was soon afraid they'd call an "undertaker."

A couple big guys with arms folded blocked my exit. Joshua offered me a seat.

Then, a balding man stuck his head in the doorway and said, "Hey kid, whoever you are, thanks for saving us the bus fare and the trouble of getting you here from the airport. I have to say you're pretty remarkable."

Then, he left.

CRAP! How did they know about my plane flight to Florida?

Jack Strauss, a.k.a. "Pete Sommers," a.k.a. "Dr. Jefferson" arrived about thirty minutes later. He hadn't changed from his sweaty clothes yet and was holding the goggles I left behind at his locker. He came in and put them on Pengrove's desk in front of me, saying, "I think you left these at the tennis club and the apple was a nice touch. We have lots to talk about. You don't have to work tonight at the Rat, do you?"

I smiled and replied, "I could check my calendar."

Joshua took out a summary sheet with the name "Houdini" printed on top.

"Got it right here, Chief!" He thumbed his way down to the heading that read, "Work Schedule." He glanced up at Strauss and commented, "Looks like he's off tonight."

During the interchange, Joshua opened the envelope I'd been delivering and found the invitation to dinner at the pizza joint.

He set it aside, remarking, "Pizza sounds good, but I think we will be ordering in tonight. Nice work on Miss Baxter's summary sheet by the way. I'll have to keep it under wraps for a while, though, or somebody might give you my job. You really are some kind of smart ass, aren't you?"

I nodded with a smile and eagerly accepted his compliment.

"Did you notice how I modified the page so that you have more information on the front side? Doesn't the new design seem more efficient?"

I had the sneaking suspicion that things weren't going to follow as well as I'd expected. It was obvious that they weren't used to having sleepovers at IPM. That afternoon I heard discussions in the hall about where to put the cots and blankets. The cleaning crew was also canceled.

Axiom One Hundred Eighteen
When apology won't help, blame the aliens!

Can you remember, as a kid, getting into such big trouble that no matter what, there wasn't going to be any way out of it? It happened when Wendell and I were having dirt-clod fights with the neighbor kids up the street. That's where you grab chunks of dirt from the edge of the driveway and fling them at each other. Chipper and Karen were standing in front of their Mom's laundry that hung on the line to dry when we began throwing these at our opponents. I remember how cool it was seeing the clods explode on the backdrop of the sheets. That was until Chip's mother came out and caught us destroying her hard work and called my Mom.

Wowza! Were we ever in for it! Mom demanded an explanation, but nothing, no nothing was going to help us escape the belt and we knew it!

Creating extra work and undue duress for a housewife was nearly an unpardonable sin. I remembered this as I realized I was about to be hung out to dry for the trouble I'd created in Paramus.

Axiom One Hundred Nineteen
Always have an endgame in mind.

They moved me to another room for an hour or so. Dr. J finally came in all cleaned up and asked if I was comfortable. He said dinner would be arriving around 6:00 p.m. Glancing at my watch, I asked if he received overtime for staying ninety minutes past his usual departure at 4:30.

"You're remarkable, Levi. Most spies keep their intel a secret, but you seem to enjoy flaunting it. I'm extremely impressed with everything you've figured out about IPM. I just wish I could say the same for my coworkers. They're extremely pissed."

I started to say something, but Strauss interrupted, "You've really brought some excitement to our office that also puts us in a bind." He looked at me dourly and continued, "You know, there could be grave circumstances." Then he changed his tone and added, "And, by the way, I had the rest of the afternoon off today for my tennis match, so if you survive, you're going to owe me when this is all finished."

I asked, "How will this all get finished?"

He was silent for a moment, opened his drawer and removed a .45 caliber, short barreled, 1911 style, semi-automatic Colt. After racking the slide, checking the hammer and flipping up the safety, he slid the pistol into a well-hidden holster inside the rear waistband of his pants. He pulled his shirt down over the concealed weapon and paced to the other side of the room as if in deep thought.

"Here's the problem, Levi. We don't know what to think about a person who has outsmarted, infiltrated, and perhaps compromised our private little world. The quandary we now face is sorting out who you are, whether or not you're working for someone else, and determining your motives." He paced back and forth, continuing, "We could interrogate you, but how would we know if you were telling the truth? We've been deliberating about your case and it looks as if it's going to be an endgame of 'trial by ordeal.' Are you familiar?"

I thought for a moment, waiting to see if he would fill in the blank. It's better not to suggest any ideas that might turn out to be worse than your opponent already had in mind.

He stared at me and continued, "'Trial by ordeal' is a very old method of determining guilt or innocence."

I asked, "Isn't that where they dunked a person underwater and if he drowned in the process, he was judged as having been innocent?"

"Exactly."

I thought I might pee my pants!

"Look! I was just trying to figure out who you were and why you were having me do all these crazy escapes."

He interrupted, "And in the process, you learned things that can only be known by our closest family members." He paused then added, "Do you speak any southeast Asian languages?"

In an attempt to add some humor and lighten the situation I replied, "Loren Ipsum dolor sit arnet consectetur adipiscing elit!"

He laughed and concluded, "I didn't really think so."

Then, Strauss got all serious, looking reflective with his hand held on his chin. He finally said, "I hope I can help you, Levi."

Was this going to turn into a good cop/bad cop scenario between him and Pengrove?

"Tomorrow you're not actually going to Orlando."

He placed a copy of the brochure I'd received regarding the marine geology work-study program on the table.

I suddenly felt nauseous.

"Instead we're providing you with a more challenging vacation destination. The location is still being worked out. I don't know if it's going to end there, but it is the next part of the plan."

Axiom One Hundred Twenty
At all cost, avoid trial by ordeal.

Joshua Pengrove entered the room and handed me a passport, which I opened and read silently with astonishment: "Adam Goodwin."

I smiled and ventured, "Hey guys, this looks just like the real thing!"

Strauss was unmoved by my levity, "We don't hand these out to just anybody, Levi. Believe me! I should admit that you really earned this. I thought from the first party in New Paltz, 'This guy, Levi, is something else!' Well congratulations! Now you've actually become someone else."

Pengrove addressed both of us, "Jacob got sick of hearing all these amazing stories about you from Josef! When he learned your score on the Dominion I.Q., test he said you must have cheated. I too dismissed the results, because I didn't think anyone with your college grades could have possibly achieved such high marks on his own. Now, however, I'm beginning to wonder."

Dr. J interjected, "Tomorrow you're going to wake up in a different world. I hope it's not the end-game, but instead, that it becomes a new beginning. Joshua, here, has his doubts, but I'm betting you aren't going to let us down!"

Sharon Baxter appeared in the room holding something small. It was shielded in her hand and hidden from my view.

She asked, "Ready?"

Dr. J said, "Not yet."

She looked at me with a fiendish smile and said, "I got the notes you dropped by this morning. What a surprise!" She asked mischievously, "You don't happen to be that guy who plays for the

212

New York Knicks, do you? It'll make my mailman jealous!" With an angry looking face, she called me a name and marched out of the room without letting me see what she held.

Everyone was missing out on the humor in all of this! I'd thought Sharon's bio was pretty, stinking funny! Well, that had backfired nicely. I guess my frontal lobe wasn't so well developed after all!

Pengrove filled the silence, "And by the way, Levi, it wasn't a pretty scene this morning when she phoned the office to question me about the papers she'd found on her car. Great job of setting me up!"

It was his second compliment. I was beginning to win him over.

Axiom One Hundred Twenty-One
Don't always try to get out of trouble.
Instead, push forward with resolve!

There was something about the grand adventure of bridge jumping that was a firm demonstration of one's commitment to the cause. Once you'd flung your body over the edge, it was a no turning back proposition. It's like when Uncle Sheldon jumped off the roof with Grandma's parasol. Even though it turned inside out and was destroyed, he proceeded full steam ahead into the driveway. Grandma became adept at mending her boys' sprained ankles, but their injuries didn't discourage gramps from also tanning their hides. Crime inevitably meets with punishment as certain as the design of the cosmos and the rising of the sun.

In the here and now, there was no chance of these guys letting me off the hook with a light slap on the back of my hands.

In the deep recesses of my mind I heard Wendell's voice of warning. "You're in for it, Levi!"

The Martin Clan were equally galvanized by a sense of unswerving resolve. When any of us was in trouble over our head, we'd proceed forward with as much energy as possible. There was no turning back. Against all odds, we played to win; especially in situations where we no longer had anything to lose.

Today, we were way beyond the point of hoping that a remorseful, tear-jerking apology might elicit compassion. Sympathy could have provided no reasonable corrective for my circumstances. Instead, it was time to work a strong punk attitude and to take it all up a few notches to turn the tomfoolery into a mind-blowing experience. I was backed into a corner with no other choice. I'd demonstrate for the folks at IPM just exactly how cunning Martins showed their friends a good time.

~ An Aside from Mom ~

Mom never gave up on anything she'd set her heart on. Much of that had to do with raising her sons. Wendell and I were hellions, born and bred living in the Martin Clan in an existence like Vikings. What we became growing up was the product of survival. Dad raised us as fighters tried and true. He warned us, "In this world, you'll face trouble, and you've got to live prepared. In fact, he wouldn't let Mom break up a fight between us and the first one that cried had to face him. Mom didn't object to us being fighters, but moreover she hoped for us to find ourselves enlisted in a greater army strengthened by the Almighty.

My little brother and I were in the midst of an all-out war scuffing it out kicking and screaming in the back yard, but Mom determined that her voice would prevail over the mayhem. She shouted at us as we duked it out, "You two had better listen to me, and listen to me now! In this world you'll face tribulation, but you need to take hold of the One who's overcome the world!"

It was enough to distract Wendell long enough for me to pop him in the eye. My brother didn't stop, but neither did Mom, "One day you're gonna' need one another so you had better get this through your thick skulls right now. You're gonna' face far greater enemies and in that day remember that the Almighty prepares a table before you in the presence of your enemies."

Mom hadn't realized it but we weren't in any disposition to listen to a sermon. He caught me in the ribs, and I curled my arms to block his fists while I caught my breath. Neither of us were letting up.

She shouted even louder, "That means no matter what it looks like, you've got to face trouble as winners who've got lots more than brute force has to offer. No matter how big or powerful any threat pretends to be, you remember and call forth the One who rules heaven and earth and live life in his power. Your will to fight alone will never be enough. When that day arrives, it's all about knowing his will for your lives and don't forget it!

Axiom One Hundred Twenty-Two
The world is your stage. The sun is your spotlight.
Love your audience and perform well!

At dinner, a group of IPMers gathered around, as I sat at a table with a box of pizza that was just out of reach; a meal prepared for me in the presence of a group of individuals, who despite my best efforts, had all become my enemies. The day had arrived and one thing was certain; I was not only going to survive, but I would move forward to carry out a greater mission. I wasn't

215

always certain if my life allowed me to be on speaking terms with the Almighty, but somehow, I felt as if he had a hand in all this and he wasn't going to fail me.

A couple of heavies were blocking the door, and we were high up on the fifth-floor, so the window wasn't a promising means of exit. Nevertheless, I might just have to take my chances.

Jack asked, "Well, Levi, I'm curious as to your greatest fear at this moment."

The punk in me came out and I was about to pour it on thick.

I smiled as I responded, "Well, first off, the way you're concealed carrying, I'm afraid you might accidentally blow a second hole in your rear end." I shook my head, "I just think it's bad form to walk around with a 1911, hot from behind."

I looked around inquisitively, feigning great care, then letting my voice trail off and leaning forward as if to express some valuable secret.

"When you sit back in a chair, the safety can get pushed down."

I whispered, "You know what could happen next?"

Straining to hear, they also bent over toward me.

As loud as I could, I shouted, "POW!"

Everyone jumped, and I thought the bald guy was going to have a heart attack.

Then, without missing a beat, I admonished, "You could lose a testicle. After that, the rest of these guys will be telling jokes about the reason you walk funny."

Nobody expected my brazen attitude or joking, and I knew right off that I was conjuring some of the effect that I hoped for. Strauss looked shocked.

Finally, he replied, "Thanks, Levi. I'll consider your advice."

For the moment, I was running the show. I shook my head, shrugged, and put on a serious look glancing from face to face.

I continued feigning deep concern, "Let's just say that I care about you 'Jack.'" I placed a heavy emphasis on his name then went on, "Or is it 'Pete' or 'Elias' or something else?"

My defiant attitude reshaped the mood in the room. Moments earlier when the interrogation had begun, the staff were confidently in control of the situation. Now there was a decided and unexpected shift. I wasn't the same golden retriever that Jack had worked with for the preceding months. He thought he had me pegged, but now, I'd taken him by surprise.

Strauss squinted and finally said, "I'm seeing a whole different side of you today, Levi."

I shrugged theatrically asking, "Oh, really? I wonder why?"

The two heavies by the door were smiling, at the irony. A captive who should otherwise have acted fearfully contrite. They knew my attempt to antagonize the head of operations was futile. The absurdity of my punk attitude proved I was an ignoramus who was probably only moments away from joining the dearly departed in the basement freezer.

Baldy observed the situation with anger and demanded, "Let's get serious, guys. And you kid, I don't like your insolence. You're running out of time fast. You need to explain what's going on before you find out personally just how a Colt .45 works!"

I replied, "Okay, I'm going to tell you everything. But, if you had just gone down to Dino's for the pizza, you would already have the answers you're looking for."

I could feel Martin instinct kicking in. "So, here's the real story. I'm going to level with you 100%. If you don't buy what I say, well then, whatever happens next is all on you!"

I frowned at the table as if I was searching my soul for a place to begin, and my audience remained silent. I thought about the bits and pieces of information I'd learned from the notes in IPM's trash.

"We've got to start somewhere, so here goes. There's a man named 'Omar' who was the point-man for a certain individual of international corporate importance. I think you know who I'm referencing here, right?"

My audience traded glances around the room but said nothing. They refocused on me.

"Omar realized that someone was following him and then later discovered that they were after his employer. Their organization's suspicion led them to seek out a topnotch, highly trained ally; with the ability to trace the roots of the intrigue. After all, there were many lives and a large amount of money at stake. Following a series of phone calls and discussions, my employer arranged for me to drop out of school at Delphi and to apply for admission to New Paltz."

I paused and looked across the table. They seemed to be hanging on every word.

"Can you pass a slice of pizza, please? I want the piece on the left. It has more pepperoni."

One of the big guys looked around for approval and then tore off a piece, put it on a paper plate, and slid it across the table. The tension in the room was palpable and mounting. Old Baldy was measurably irritated by my interruption of the story. I decided to kick things into high gear.

"I realize that you want to know this, so I'm going to just tell you straight out. I work for Ambercrombie Relations Associates. The world renown ARA Corporation is a front that actually exists as a tactical counterintelligence agency who hires freelancers..."

Pengrove abruptly interrupted and cut me off, "This is a stinking load of crap! He began swearing and said, This kid is a *&%$# liar! He's never had interactions of any kind with Omar or anyone in that part of the world! And Ambercrombie, a front? Huh?"

He stared me down, but I pretended to be more interested in what I was eating.

The bald man admonished Pengrove with a dour look of reprimand for the interruption.

Trial by fire and the swoosh of the belt had taught the Martin cousins more than a few lessons about working the crowd. I'd touched a nerve and forced Pengrove's hand. That was a good sign to keep moving forward.

I smacked my lips and moved my tongue awkwardly as if trying to free a slab of cheese stuck to my teeth. I looked up with surprise at everyone as if suddenly having discovered that I wasn't alone.

I glanced at Pengrove and asked tersely, "You done?"

219

He was fuming, but I was about to pour some gasoline on his fire.

It was an intense moment. I felt everyone's eyes glued to me. A certain level of apprehension was palpable in the air. They waited for what I'd say next.

Baldy asked, "Well?"

I raised my hand and gestured forward and nodded theatrically as if I were about to continue; kind of eyeing Pengrove as if to ask, "You gonna' be quiet now and let me finish?"

The room traded glances again, and you could have heard a pin drop.

Finally, I continued, "Okay then, I'll tell you what we really need here. It should be obvious, and so, I'm only going to say it once."

Baldy replied, "Go ahead."

Everyone got quiet and leaned in to listen.

"Well, to be honest, I'm thinking that this pizza really deserves a can of Mtn. Dew. What do you guys think? Would someone mind springing for a can from the vending machine in the front hall?"

The bald guy's declining demeanor, mannerisms, and language betrayed the fact that he was near to losing his temper.

"Look, kid, you better cut the bull crap and start talking some sense, here and now!"

Axiom One Hundred Twenty-Three
Divide in order to conquer.

I had them going with a wedge set in place between Pengrove and Shiny Top and built on the momentum.

"So, my name isn't really 'Adam Goodwin.'"

Pengrove couldn't restrain himself and mumbled, half under his breath, "No kidding!"

Now, I imitated Old Baldy. I paused, raised my eyebrows, and stared at him condescendingly.

Then, I went on, "Neither is my name 'Levi Martin.'"

Pengrove rolled his eyes and sighed before Baldy silenced him again with another terse glance.

The older man ordered me, "Continue!"

Every intelligent Viking understood that when he was up against an immovable force, facing impossible odds, and when finding he was insurmountably out-numbered, his only hope in overcoming was to convince his adversary that his army was larger than life and mightier than power itself. At this point, survival hinged on a battle of wits. That's right where I was with IPM, as the lie of lies proceeded forth from my lips.

I continued, "Omar realized that a guy named 'Mark' had him under surveillance. He went to pick up his employer's kid from school, all the while, making certain that Mark was watching him. Omar wasted about thirty minutes to give his employer's men time to search Mark's apartment. They discovered enough information to lead them back to IPM." I took a chance with what followed and added, "Oh, yeah, and Mark was later taken captive. He should have been more careful!"

I had taken a big risk in connecting Mark to Omar, but since the papers from Strauss' trash were bunched together it seemed as if the two situations might be related. I shook my head and looked around the room, studying their reactions.

It sounded so plausible that even I began to believe what I was saying. "Boondoggle" might as well have been my middle name!

Axiom One Hundred Twenty-Four
If you resort to open deception, lie big!

"So, let me get to the point. The actual reason I'm here today eating your pizza..."

I paused to chomp off a bite and ate it with my mouth open, nonsensically bobbing my head with each chew, staring nonchalantly off into space.

"...is because of this carefully orchestrated plan."

I nodded at myself in a showy way, theatrically raising my eyebrows and took another sip of soda and chewed some more.

I heard Mom's voice in my mind, "Eat with your mouth closed!"

They all looked at each other incredulously. I hoped I was further angering them, by playing the role of a stupid punk.

"Today, you have become erroneously convinced that I'm your captive. By this time, however," I chewed some more and raised my hand up at the clock, then continued, "your building is surrounded. The reason I came here was to offer you terms on behalf of my employer. What do you think? Can we strike a deal?"

You should've seen the looks on their faces! I took another bite and let them chew on this new revelation.

"We can get Mark back stateside in about three days if you decide to comply." After pausing, I suggested, "Or, we can blow the lid off of what you guys are actually up to around here."

Nobody was saying anything, so I pushed the Pengrove button again.

"Look, there's no reason we need to get stalemated at this point. Let me provide a little more incentive."

I glanced up at Joshua and stared until our eyes had met for several uncomfortable seconds. I could tell he hated my guts.

"By the way, sir, I want to assure you that Alfred and Elizabeth are safe, and I'm not going to let anything happen to them; but only so long as the rest of these guys cooperate."

Now, Pengrove didn't know what to think. How did I know his parents' names? If I knew who they were, however unlikely it seemed, perhaps they really were in some danger. With that, he flipped his lid and blew a gasket! After shouting several curses at me, he slammed the file folder he was holding down on the table, threw his hands up, and stormed out of the room.

Jack Strauss imposed himself upon the moment and looked straight at Old Baldy. He ordered everyone else, "Okay, it's time for a break." Then, he glared at me with exasperation, "Levi, Adam, Mystery Kid..." He waved his hand at me, "...finish that pizza, while we go for a walk."

All of them left the room for a powwow in the hallway. The tone of their voices was heated. There was disagreement among them as they debated my story in hushed shouts. I had the impression that Pengrove was becoming more like my Mom; wanting to rip my arms off and beat me to death with the bloody limbs.

It was the first time I'd found myself alone and probably the only chance for an escape. Seconds ticked by. I swiftly scooted my chair over and swung the fifth-floor window wide open and looked downward. I counted the cost, and a jump from this height would cost a broken leg or worse. I stuck my finger in the pizza, covering it with gooey tomato paste and wrote on the glass:

"Thanks for the pizza! Bye! ☺ Houdini."

I pursed my lips and remarked to myself and the angels, "This had better work!"

Axiom One Hundred Twenty-Five
Become proficient in the arts and methods of rock climbing.

Moments later, Jack reentered the room saying, "Okay, Levi..." His voice was suddenly interrupted by his own stunned silence. He looked around and saw the table, the empty chair, the open window, and the message. He realized I was gone. The papers that had been neatly arranged in the file folder Joshua Pengrove had slammed down on the table were now blowing around on the lawn outside, fifty or sixty feet below.

Strauss began swearing, then he shouted, "I can't believe it!"

Pengrove ran in, saw the obvious, and asked, "Where the hell is he?" They put two and two together, then Baldy exploded shouting orders, "Everyone outside! Get down there! Find him, now!"

The hallway erupted into chaos.

One of the big guys who'd been guarding the door previously, said, "Jumped five stories and survived? Yep, he's

224

'Houdini' alright!" Voices faded with the sound of feet scurrying toward the stairs.

When I thought it was safe, I released myself from the chimney hold below the table top and dropped to the floor. I'd suspended myself there to hide, forcing pressure from my hands and feet on the lip of the skirt on all four sides. It's a good thing that I was so stinking skinny. I peeked out the doorway. When the coast was clear, I crept across the hall and slipped inside that office. I needed a few seconds to regroup and think of an escape plan from the building.

I hadn't noticed Sharon Baxter who'd been working quietly behind the large lateral file cabinet. I'd moved around the desk in order to shield myself from anyone's view in the hall. I worked hard to control my breathing when the woman startled me.

"Oh, there you are, Levi." Before I had time to think, she jammed something into my left shoulder. I felt a painfully sharp prick, and I grabbed for my arm as I turned toward her. It only took a split second, and I felt woozy, and then the room began to wobble and spin. I slowly lowered myself and merged with the floor. I half watched and half-heard her at the doorway alerting her associates, "He's in here! Hey, guys! I found him!" She looked at me and remarked smugly, "He who laughs first, laughs last." Hadn't Durlong mentioned that before too? I think she was smiling, but the individual features of her face were blurring together. For the first time, she appeared to be strangely attractive. I mumbled, "David Jeffreys never should've let a pretty chick like you get away!"

A moment later, Old Baldy stormed back inside. In exasperation, he shouted something at me. But he'd said it so fast

I couldn't keep up with what he was saying. The room was fading in and out of view. I could barely make out his shape from the pool of slobber that had gathered around my cheek and was oozing back into my left eye.

As Pengrove and Strauss settled in behind him, he pointed down at me and said, "He says he knows 'Omar?' Well then, send his smart ass off to Bangkok!"

The last thing I remember as I desperately attempted to remain conscious was pointing toward Sharon Baxter.

I asked, "Do you think I could still purchase the mimeograph machine?"

Epilogue

Oh, and there is one more thing I know some of you are probably still wondering about: I checked it out and Psycho-Joe had chased me a total of 5.7 miles.

To be continued...

These Are the Real Stories

We use props, artifacts, create diversions, and support all of it with misinformation. We do it through friendships, liaisons, and partnerships. Falsehood, pretense, and flattery, couched in sincerity, with the ostensible desire to help, together contrived with effective formulas, make our operatives appear as each target's last hope. Disruption of trust, money, relationships, and information motivate reactionary, defensive, shortsighted decisions. As guessing replaces rational deduction, anger, desperation, and malice mix with a sense of abandonment, resulting in the self-fulfilling prophecy of irreversible doom. Ultimately, wickedness embraces its companions: fear, frustration, weakness, and worse. Malevolence finds its ultimate embrace in the grip of the Almighty.

When your world seems to be collapsing around you, before you react, make certain that you're not the victim of a mind game!

Axiom Seven Hundred Twenty-Six
Always provide more than one means of contact.

To be kept in the know regarding new publications or other cool stuff, send a note to:

adammichaelgoodwin@gmail.com

adammichaelgoodwin@yahoo.com

Also, let me know if you're interested in becoming a spy. Serious candidates must provide a complete resume listing all aliases, covert operations involvement, and summaries of detailed professional experiences. One never knows if IPM is hiring ;-)

Made in the USA
Coppell, TX
21 June 2021